HOW TO GET AN EDUCATION

HOW TO GET AN EDUCATION

Stories

Bhisham Bherwani

ELBORO

HOW TO GET AN EDUCATION

ISBN: 978-1-7379274-0-2

Published in New York by Elboro Press

Elboro Press books may be purchased in bulk for educational, business or sales promotional use. Please address enquiries to:

office@elboropress.com

First Edition, 2022 – First Printing

Thou shalt not do as the dean pleases,
Thou shalt not write thy doctor's thesis
On education.

—W. H. Auden

CONTENTS

Foreword

A volume of linked stories is a special genre all in itself, having the sustained engagement of a novel, and the curvature and concentration of short fiction. The short story must do a lot fast, wasting not a syllable, intimating more than is said or described, often with the cadence of a poem. In this collection, *How to Get an Education*, we can see some of the themes, deepened and distilled with maturing art, that characterized Bhisham Bherwani's contributions to writing workshops I presided over at Cornell University some years ago. There was one memorable piece about a journalist covering the scandals and extravagant practices of Bombay's decadent upper classes, others of rich teenagers driving their parents' luxury cars and experimenting with drugs and illicit liquor.

In each segment of this volume, Bherwani creates a special sense of place and time, connecting the reader and the characters to different periods, from preschool and prep school with an insufferable headmaster, rebellious teenagers, and wealthy friends caught up in the drug culture, to later careers in finance and academia. Bherwani's fiction is enhanced by an acute sense of atmosphere, architecture, urban landscape, and exact gradations of wealth.

A motif found throughout this collection is brotherhood, the significance of filiation. One of the most poignant sections is the portrayal of an afflicted brother who alternates between docility and violent rage, and the exhaustion of the mother who is the caregiver. The story makes palpable the tensions within the family, in the life of a teenager who hopes to escape, through music and drugs, the confusions, stifled aspirations.

Much of Bherwani's work dramatizes the conflicts and combinations of menace and intimacy. At the center of this series of stories is the account, set in Europe, mostly Germany, of Gabriele, beautiful former something—friend? lover?—of the narrator. At a colorful reunion the question is asked: why was the relationship broken off abruptly and completely years before? It is a mystery, since the narrator and Gabriele, as they meet again, share so many tastes and enthusiasms, and are still drawn to each other. "Mein Bruder?" is an eloquent, richly crafted narrative with an unforeseen ending, the mystery to further unravel in the sequel story, "Mein Bruder."

Bherwani's fiction is global in the best sense, taking place across continents, across cultures, decades, across strata of wealth, employment, and education. As the title implies, education is life itself, with all the anguish, pleasure, disappointment, learning, and irony we might expect. Looming over each section is the cruel legacy of the British Raj, and the tragic Partition of India. The history of India and the West is understood as original sin, yet that history yields a colorful, multicultural aftermath, incorporating the worlds of high finance, with brinksmanship and risk, fine wines and cuisines, school days, love, loss of friends, the poetry of memory, and challenges of scholarship and interpreting history. Bherwani demonstrates a command of the intricacies of Wall Street, but even deeper knowledge of kinship and rivalry in the financial trading community. In this fiction, the past collides with the present, reflecting the follies of the young as they confront complex legacies.

Throughout these stories, the author displays an eye for significant detail, elusive nuances of character and heritage, while exploring divided allegiances. In Bherwani's work, past and present crash and overlap. Transitions are painful, yet occasions of opportunity, education. Like the films of the character Aantya Huq, these stories are both a record of the larger shifts of history and the wrenching, intimate unfoldings of particular lives.

Robert Morgan

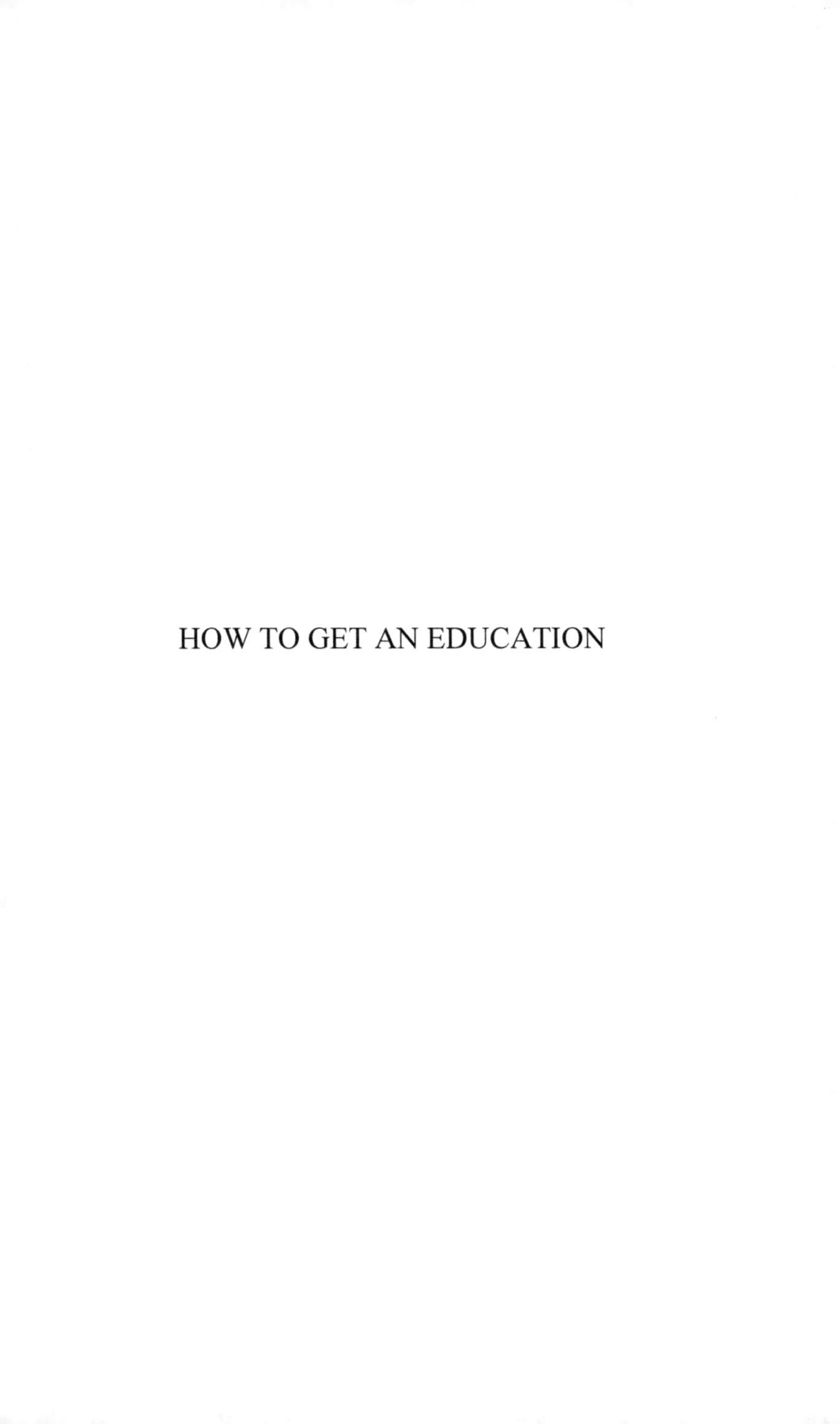

HOW TO GET AN EDUCATION

Occidens et orientis
qui hic sunt.

East and west
are one here.

I switched off the microphone. From the wings of the stage, I glanced down the hall at the students lined up in rows of single file, the shorter boys in front, the taller ones behind. They were dressed in the school uniform: cotton short-sleeve white shirts and navy-blue khakis, starched and pressed, silk burgundy and navy-blue repp ties, black leather belts and black dress shoes, polished to sparkle.

The teachers, well groomed and conservatively attired—the men in trousers, long-sleeve shirts, and ties, the women in dresses or saris—stood along the walls between the slatted double doors on both sides. They sang, too, but more earnestly than the boys, the men's Adam's apples rattling, the women's heads swaying.

The tempo picked up.

Habemus sub pédibus nostris
totius mundi.

We have the whole world
under our feet.

The hall was large, its ceilings twenty feet high, the bottom half of the walls painted an ugly glossy green, the top half an ugly glossy beige. Directly below where I stood, angled toward the audience, was a grand piano, a John Broadwood & Sons as old as the school, brought in shortly after its founding by ship from England. It was being played by Mrs. Munro, my English teacher, also the school's drama instructor. Beside her stood a student in thick black glasses, turning and holding in place the pages of the score propped up on the music rack. Now and then, Mrs. Munro deliberately lifted her hands, fat fingers poised in the air in their arrangement from the last chord, her torso recoiling, her neck arced so far back I was sure our eyes would meet. But hers remained ecstatically shut. She seemed to smell and savor the fading, floating notes as they drifted over her bosom to her nose, before she descended to the piano and continued playing.

To my right, at the lectern, stood Mr. Thomas, the principal, a somber figure in a black suit, a black tie, and a black cassock. He observed the teachers as they, in turn, observed the boys, alert to any breach of the ceremony's solemnity. The melody turned sad—"O O O Christ / We are your grist…"—before, after a few strains, picking up again—"*Studia gloria! Ludis gloria!* Honor in studies! Honor in sports!" It ended in a war cry, the music suspended and the boys shouting, "We are the New Cantuarians! The finest men of the Orient!"

Mr. Thomas smiled.

I switched on the microphone.

He read a passage from the Bible. It was something about the Lord's greatness and how we'd all be smarter if we listened to Him, no questions asked. He'd make us wise and honest, pave the way for us to a great future, to great fortunes. Then, as everyone started to sing the hymn of the day, I switched off and started to dismantle the equipment.

The assembly ended. The students, in order, went to their classrooms. I lingered after everyone left, locking up the amplifier, the microphones, and the accessories, turning off the lights and fans, hovering at the water fountains, and generally loitering around the building before I made my way, reluctantly, to class.

*

The New Cantuarians were the students and alumni of the New Canterbury School. Before being admitted seven years earlier, I had to memorize its history and its song. The history was etched in stone in the vestibule, the song on a brass plate outside the hall.

An arm of the Canterbury Grammar School in England, New Canterbury was established in 1857 in Bombay following the Indian Mutiny, with the aim "to inculcate, among the Far-Flung Boys of Our Colony, and select Gifted and Industrious Natives, the Sacred Virtues of the Enlightened Occident; to instruct in the Orient a Race of Men with Knowledge and Christian Values and Principles and Codes befitting Honorable Service to the King."

This year was special: the hundred-and-twenty-fifth anniversary of the school, or—as Jamshed told me—its quasquicentennial.

Jamshed had an interesting vocabulary and knew interesting facts, but was an even worse student than I was. He was known to have six or seven private tutors who made sure he more or less passed each year.

"I like that you wear your hair long," he said one afternoon, palms on the side of the wooden table where I sat

5

eating lunch alone. He slid onto the bench opposite mine. We had never talked before. "I like that you wear red sneakers."

I swallowed the food in my mouth, not quite sure what to say. "I hate short hair," I said. "I hate real shoes. They hurt, especially chukkas."

Everyone knew Jamshed. His father's and his grandfather's photos, and even his great-grandfather's portrait, regularly appeared in newspapers and magazines. They were a family of industrialists, noted philanthropists for five or six generations. He was driven to and from school by a uniformed chauffeur in a shiny Mercedes, windows tinted black, always rolled up. I had heard that, since the previous year, when we were fourteen, he had a girlfriend four years older than he. She would, at first, drive him out at nights. But he managed in two weeks to get a driver's license and would then drive her. But now she was at a famous college in America.

Like everyone else in school, Jamshed knew why I volunteered backstage, or, rather, why I had been volunteered for backstage chores by an indignant Mr. Thomas, and why I had been precluded from the assembly for the two years since he took over the school. Mr. Thomas was a retired serviceman—a vice admiral of the Indian Navy— and an active Anglican clergyman. Called a man of God by the preachers who visited each term, he was a despot with a crewcut, a bushy mustache, and a square jaw who, though humorless with students, smoked Dunhills and entertained and laughed with dignitaries in his office all day. He had been recruited, it was said, to lead an Indian Royal Navy fleet for the Allies in the Second World War, but the conflict ended as the fleet was about to leave port.

Within a few weeks, he had had enough of my violations

of the dress code, which upon his arrival he had printed, with illustrations, including instructions on how to tie a Windsor knot, on the inside front cover of the school's notebooks. He had had enough of my grades. He had a letter sent the previous year to my parents from the vice principal, who, two weeks later, ushered my mother and me to the admiral's office.

"Why can't he be like everyone else?" he asked her, the rosewood-paneled office smoky and smelling of tobacco.

She thought for a moment. The reflection of a banker's lamp flooded his polished mahogany desk. "He's creative," she said, staring at the puddle of light.

"Where's his father?"

"At work," she said softly, looking up.

"What does he do?"

"He's a businessman."

He looked at her curiously.

"He's had three warnings already. That's grounds for dismissal."

"I'm sorry," she said.

He turned to me. "If it weren't for Mrs. Munro's recommendation to go easy on you," he said, "I'd expel you right now. She said you like Shakespeare. It so happens, I have a corner for Shakespeare in my heart."

I was quiet. I didn't know he had a heart. I didn't know I liked Shakespeare that much. But I knew no one else liked him.

"Is that true?" he asked.

My mother slipped her foot toward mine and tapped it.

"Yes, sir," I said, "I like Shakespeare."

She tapped it harder.

"I love him," I said. "I love Shakespeare, sir."

"What else do you like?"

I again didn't know what to say. I knew everybody loved music. "I like music," I said.

"The loud stuff from America or real music? Do you like the school's music?"

"Yes, sir," I said. "I love it. I love the school's music."

I hated it.

He leaned back and stared at the space between my mother and me. He squinted.

"I'll put you to work on a probationary basis," he said turning to me on his swiveling, cozy leather chair and leaning forward, "where you can stop being an eyesore at assembly. But if you fail another class, that'll be it." He leaned back again and looked at me. "You can go."

I stood up to leave, hoping the probation would last forever and I would never again have to line up for assembly, even though the back of the stage smelled of urine, including mine. The hot draft from outside struck me as I opened the door of the air-conditioned office. When I looked back, he had turned his attention to my mother. "For someone from the wrong side of the tracks," he said as I stepped out, "he should consider himself fortunate to be in the only school on the continent with Latin and Greek."

"You hate short hair," said Jamshed, "and you hate real shoes. Is there anything you like?" I took another bite of my sandwich. I shrugged.

"Do you like Shakespeare?" he asked. He had changed his voice to a grown-up's.

I looked at him. He had curly black hair, a small flat nose, and lively eyes. He looked well-fed. He was smiling. I beamed. "Yes, sir," I said, swallowing my food, "I love Shakespeare."

We laughed.

After that, we talked every day.

*

My father owns the best liquor business in Bombay. I'm proud of him. His clients include Bollywood actors, local politicians, and tax officers. Even the most powerful pimp from Kamathipura, the red-light district, is his customer. He has a large store off the lobby, next to the famous Shore Leave discotheque, in the five-star Mariner InterContinental Hotel. It's cash-only, and for special orders—a few cases of something not legally or easily available, something custom-made or banned or with restrictive levies—he charges a premium. He works late, taking orders after the store closes, after midnight, at the door from his office in the back that opens onto a small alcove barely noticeable to passers-by outside, off to the side and behind a pillar where the wide corridor that connects the boutiques to the lobby turns in the other direction.

On the 125th Inauguration Day, halfway through the term, an envelope from the principal's office for my parents was delivered to me during Mrs. Kumar's mathematics class in the afternoon. She was short, could reach just over halfway up the blackboard, and had a high-pitched voice. She called out my name. She stood on her toes and looked around.

I don't believe in God, but I thank Him for one thing: for making me tall. Each year I was assigned a seat in the back of the class. Melvin, who sat to my left, woke me up. I quickly sat up and raised my hand: "Here, ma'am." She placed the envelope on the desk at the head of the row in which I sat. The envelope, desk by desk, percolated to me, each boy examining it, front and back, before passing it to the boy behind him. Paper-clipped on the envelope was a note for me: the admiral wanted to see me after school.

Mrs. Kumar glared at me, then continued. The blackboard was filled with numbers, except of course the top part beyond her reach, which was blank.

After school, Melvin gave me his shoes and went home in my sneakers. I went to the locker room to adjust my tie. The teams were changing for cricket practice, singing "Louie, Louie." *Flush hard*, someone had scribbled above the urinal, *it's a long way to the school cafeteria kitchen sink*. The admiral's assistant, a retired junior serviceman who sat outside the principal's office, stopped me as I was about to knock. "He's busy," he said. "It's Inauguration Day."

"He called for me," I said.

"Don't be impertinent," he said. "The admiral doesn't have time for trivialities."

I raced downstairs. The school bus had just started to leave. I ran and caught it, the driver scowling as I leaped inside. I sat by the window in the back and looked out. The Victorian, dark gray stone façade, the Gothic arches, the gargoyles on the roof receded. The bus turned onto the main road and merged into the rush-hour traffic.

At my stop at Breach Candy, I was blinded for a moment by the glare from the late afternoon sun reflected on the sea. I walked past the grand Lincoln House, the US Consulate General's headquarters, inland toward the building where I live. As I approached, I heard my brother's screams piercing the windows of our thirteenth-floor apartment and echoing all around the neighborhood. Pedestrians stopped and looked about. My doorman stepped out of the lobby and looked up.

I heard my brother above the loud ding-dong of the doorbell. My mother opened the door. She was hysterical.

"He's having one of his tantrums," she said. "I took him

to the psychiatrist this morning and gave him the new medicines, but he's having one of his tantrums again."

I hugged her and walked in.

"I locked him in his room," she said.

I heard his head pound—*thud*—against the wall.

She held out her swollen hands—scratched and bit into—to show me the bloodstains. "I don't know what to do," she said. "I don't know what to do."

She was breathless. Her hair clung to her sweaty forehead and fell over her eyes. I wiped her brow with my palm.

Tears flowed out of my mother's eyes. One trickled down her cheek, fell on her knuckles, and turned red. It rolled down the back of her raised hand, over her turgid veins, to her wrist, adorned with bangles.

Those were her once delicate, pristine hands.

We stood outside my brother's room. We heard him scream and slap his cheeks and we heard his head pound—*thud, thud, thud*—against the furniture. We stood at the door until he quieted, exhausted by his spasm of violence. Then we unlocked him.

He gasped and sobbed quietly.

*

I took a public bus to the Bombay Central station, a train to the suburbs, and an auto-rickshaw, past the beautiful churches in Bandra, to the Mariner InterContinental Hotel. In my hand I had the envelope from school.

My father was billing some customers when I entered. I walked behind the counter and stood beside him. Then, as the clients left, I handed him the envelope. "How did you get here?" he asked. He was not angry.

"By train," I said. "Alone."

The letter was about my poor academic performance and about my disregard for the school's code of conduct. It was a warning about probable expulsion.

My father said don't worry, he'd get me a private tutor. He was confident, he said, of my intellectual abilities. He told me I was hardworking and talented.

I told him I wanted to be a psychiatrist. He kissed me on the cheek.

While he attended to customers, I sat on a tall stool off to the side of the counter reading *Oliver Twist*.

The storefront is a large room with shelves on all sides stocked with bottles of local beers, Portsmouth Lager, Bombay Stout, Heidelberg Pilsner; brandies; gins; vodkas; ports. A column of shelves hides a door that opens to the office, where my father derives most of his profit from merchandise he doesn't stock. It's unlicensed, smuggled from America and Europe through Africa on merchant ships, delivered to customers the day it arrives onshore.

Behind the office's steel desk, a hidden recess in the wall is stocked with cases of dirt-cheap grain alcohol, in bottles with insignias of distilleries that don't exist. Their labels, their names, change each month. Its clientele is low-level politicians and tax officers and die-hard alcoholics.

Later that evening, a couple staggered into the shop. The man wore black pleated pants, a black shirt, and a white tie, and the girl, around whose waist he'd wrapped his arm, a short, black skirt and a black top that ran over her breasts and under her shoulders. Gold chains around his neck hung out over his shirt. He could have been someone I'd seen on screen, a showy villain in a local movie. He picked out two bottles of whiskey and paid for them. He asked my father for a cigarette.

My father didn't have one. He didn't smoke.

"You're a bastard," the man shouted. "A bastard."

He was cursing my father. He was staring at me with his bloodshot eyes, pointing at my father, and swearing. I walked up to the counter and stood in front of my father.

"You're a fucking bastard."

"Papa."

My father placed his hands on my shoulders.

The girl laughed. Her breasts heaved.

"Bastard," he shouted staggering to the door with the girl, turning around and swearing as they stumbled out.

After they left, I waited in the lobby while my father closed the shop. Music pulsed from the discotheque. When its doors opened, blue, red, and yellow strobe lights swept across the marble floor and over me.

*

A few weeks after I met Jamshed, shortly before the preliminary tests, which preceded the year-end final exams by a month, he picked me up at six in the evening. We had become good friends. He'd recounted for me his adventures, told me about the massage parlors in Bangkok, the Reeperbahn in Hamburg, Forty-Second Street in New York City, Bourbon Street in New Orleans. He was always allowed a leave of absence from school. Travel like Jamshed's, the admiral emphasized in his speeches, would provide us with an education to appreciate for the rest of our lives, an education that would serve us well in our paths to success, which was guaranteed, because we were special, we were New Cantuarians.

A red Peugeot had pulled over in front of me where I stood at the gate of my building. I didn't see Jamshed behind the tinted rolled-up windows. "Don't be afraid to

13

come in," he said, opening the passenger-side door, "I have a license." The greasy paper plate on which he'd written my address at lunch sat on the dashboard; a lit cigarette sat in the ashtray. "Where should we go?"

"I thought we were going to your father's office to work on the essay. You were going to show me his computer. I've never seen a computer. Except in movies."

"It's too early. Let's drive. Let's go to Counter Point Records. I hear they have new cassettes and LPs from America."

It was dusk. The days had started to shorten, the evenings to cool. Windows rolled down, we drove south on Marine Drive along Backbay, the sea still, the sun skimming the horizon, toward the Victoria Terminus station, then past the Bombay Stock Exchange around Horniman Circle, turning onto a side street. Colonial buildings with grand facades and large interiors surrounded us. The businesses and banks had closed, the commuters gone home. At the end of the block was the main road, where the two-way traffic still hummed. A store was open a few yards ahead of where we parked; its fluorescent light spilled through its glass doors onto the curb.

Jamshed spoke with a salesman, who brought him a small stack of records. We took them to a listening room. He selected an LP and placed it on the gramophone. "This is supposed to be very good."

"How do you know?"

"Mira told me."

"Who's Mira."

"My girlfriend. She's in America. Do you know Saint Sebastian Junior College?"

"Yes, it's near here, on the main road."

"She studied there."

The record spinning, he turned on the amplifier and turned the volume up, then higher, to its maximum. He listened intently to the first song. I read the graffiti on the wall behind the red faux-leather sofa: *Saint Sebastian girls suck cock*, someone had scribbled; someone else, *Sebastian boys lend ass*; someone else, *Virginity is like a balloon: one prick and its gone*.

"Do you like it?"

"Yes."

"Here," he said, giving me the jacket: Led Zeppelin's *Coda*.

"You've never been here?"

"No."

"What do you do in the evenings?"

"Homework."

"What?" The song had become louder.

I raised my voice. "Homework."

"That's it?"

It was loud, we were shouting. "I help my mother with the housework."

"You don't have servants?"

"No.

"Why?"

"We've tried."

"What happened?"

"Nothing."

He looked confused. "Well," I said, "my brother drives them crazy."

"Why?"

"Never mind."

The speakers had started to screech. He turned to the amplifier, lowered the volume a little. He perused the other record jackets, taking his time with each.

We heard the whole album. By the time we left the room, the store, empty of customers, had closed and was half-shuttered. But the register had been kept open for Jamshed. He bought the LPs.

The streetlights were on. We drove further south, to Kala Ghoda, past the Prince of Wales Museum, its white, marble dome rising above the palm trees; past Astor Cinema, where *The French Lieutenant's Woman* was being replaced on the billboard by *Chariots of Fire*; around the Wellington Fountain toward the Taj Hotel. He turned onto the road behind it, drove down some blocks, past the Salvation Army building, and double-parked at an intersection with a side street.

"Wait," he said. The car's engine running, he walked across the street to a shuttered kiosk plastered with flyers advertising baby milk. He knocked. The shutter clanked. He whispered something loudly, knocked again. A light turned on from inside, skimming the edges of the shutter. It was raised. In front was a glass display with chocolate bars and cigarettes. Jamshed spoke with the vendor who, in a white undershirt, was yawning and rubbing his eyes.

Jamshed walked back to the car, looking at the buildings behind him. We drove down the side street and stopped at the middle of the block. He turned off the engine. To our right was an empty park, its gates shut. Tall banyan trees arched over its periphery. Stray leaves and flowers littered the pavement.

Jamshed unwrapped a sachet of newsprint he held in his hand. Inside was a piece of folded metal foil. He unfolded it to reveal two dark blobs. He opened the glove compartment, removed from it a matchbox and a screwdriver, and tossed one blob inside.

He removed a cigarette from the pack in his breast

pocket, teased out the tobacco from it using the screwdriver, and placed it, hollowed, in his mouth. He struck a match, lifted up the foil, and held the flame under the blob. It smoldered.

He threw the matchstick in the ashtray and squeezed the blob between forefinger and thumb. It crumbled. He mixed it with the tobacco. "See," he said, holding out the foil to me.

"What is it?"

"Medicine."

He sucked the powdery blend into the empty cigarette, which filled, and tapped its filter on the dashboard to pack it. He stuffed it, folding the foil to slide the residue in. He held it up at arm's length in the direction of the streetlamp and screwed up his eyes.

Placing the cigarette between his lips, he lit it. He inhaled. He exhaled. He took another drag.

"Here," he said. "Try it."

"No."

"It won't kill you."

"Listen, I have to go. I'll take a taxi."

"It's fine, I'll drop you off." He took another drag. "You know," he said, "I'm worried about you."

"Why?"

"You seem depressed."

"I'm okay."

He lowered his backrest and reclined. Sweat filmed his brow, but he looked unruffled otherwise. He took another drag.

"How is it?" I asked.

"Very good," he said. He held the cigarette up in front of me.

"Try it. It's good for you. Everyone in school's done it."

"No," I said. But I took it. I held it up toward the street-lamp as he had.

"Close your eyes and do it," he said.

I closed my eyes and took a drag. I coughed.

"I can't smoke this."

He laughed. "Try again. Slowly. *Slooowly.*"

I took another drag.

"Good," he said, taking the cigarette from my hand. He took a drag. "Tell me, why do you go to school?" He passed me the cigarette.

"Why? To get an education." I took a drag.

"You have ambitions?"

"I want to be a psychiatrist."

"If you want to be a psychiatrist, you're going to have to repeat the year."

"No, I was promoted last year." I took another drag and handed him the cigarette.

"This is this year. You're failing everything." He took a drag. "Except Latin and Greek." He was teasing: there was no grade, no test, no final exam, for the class. Everyone passed.

"I don't understand anything Simon says," I said. "I don't mean the Latin and Greek. I mean the English, too."

"Be appreciative," he said, sitting up. "Simon's the only teacher in the world who knows elementary Latin and Greek." He leaned forward and knocked the ash into the ashtray. "I mean," he said, "he's the only Latin and Greek teacher in the world who knows no more Latin and Greek than elementary." He leaned back again. "And he knows more Latin and Greek than English."

I laughed. He was quiet, looked serious. "He does it for free, almost," he said. "He lives in school and he's paid a stipend, more than he'd get back home in England."

"How do you know?"

He looked at me incredulously. "Where have you been?" he said. "The admiral's my dad's golf partner."

"Latin and Greek are useless."

"Yes, but…" He pouted his lips and blew smoke rings. "They're useless, but… but half the school board, through a complicated arrangement with the church and the government, is still British." He looked at me. "If the admiral had his way, he'd bring in all the teachers from England." He took another drag. "Here…" I took the cigarette. He placed his hands behind his head. He exhaled. More rings drifted to the windshield. "In fact, if he had his way, all the students, too."

I took a drag. The cigarette was down to a stub. I handed it to him. He held it in his hand as he spoke, circled it above his face, as if thinking and explaining something important. "But he won't have his way, because half the school board, which includes my dad, is Indian." He took a drag and coughed. He sat up, extending his arm to the ashtray. "Just like him: half British, half Indian. But the Jesus gene's the dominant one." He extinguished the cigarette.

"I don't believe in Jesus," I said. "I hate hymns."

"I don't believe in Jesus either," he said, "but if the fucking leeches had made the school coed, I'd sing to him even if it wasn't the rule." He said it sadly, wistfully. He sighed.

He took out another cigarette from the box. He looked thoughtful again. His brow furrowed. "You know *Trombiculidae*, from Martin and Martin?" He started hollowing out the cigarette, as before.

"Who're Martin and Martin?"

"They're the authors of your biology textbook."

"I hate biology."

He was quiet, focused on making another joint.

"It's the fancy word for chiggers," he said after a long pause, placing the new joint in his mouth. His face lit up behind the flame as he brought a match to it. He inhaled. He exhaled. "They're unwanted," he said, flinging the match into the ashtray, "but they get into your skin anyway. They can't help it. That's how Jesus, or Jesus's dad, made them. They're not easily removed and not without aftereffects— rashes, etcetera—and you feel them for a while after you're rid of them."

I thought for a moment. I chuckled. He passed me the joint. I took a drag. "Why didn't you go to a coed school like Davies Academy?" I asked.

"My dad's a New Cantuarian, like his dad, like his dad's dad."

"You're trapped." I passed him the joint.

He took another drag. Then, without exhaling, another. He slumped back. He looked up at the roof of the car. He exhaled. The inside had filled up with smoke. He lowered the window an inch and looked out through the open slit. "No," he said. "I'll escape."

I reclined. I was comfortable. He gave me the joint. I took a drag, then held it between my fingers, my arms crossed.

I screamed.

Grotesque insect-like creatures, first one, then many, were multiplying before me. They had Simon's face, fat and round, but smaller, Simon's head, the same blond hair, but with antennas. They wore the round glasses he sometimes wore, and grinned, teeth showing, as he sometimes did. They started crawling up my arms. I slapped my arms, left and right, right and left, writhing and screaming.

"What're you doing?" said Jamshed.

"I'm killing them."

He shoved me.

"What's wrong with you? There's nothing on your arms."

I held up my arms and looked at them. He was correct. The Simon-bugs had disappeared.

"Where's the joint?" he screamed.

"Fuck," I screamed. I lifted myself up to see if it had fallen on the seat. I leaned forward and looked around my feet.

"It's here," said Jamshed, lifting it off the edge of the gearbox. "Take another drag. Maybe you're imagining things because it's your first time."

I was breathless. I took another drag. I expected the bugs to return, but they didn't. Then I stopped expecting them and started to feel everything was alright. I lay back again. The streets, the buildings, the stray pedestrians outside were dissolving into nothing. I even forgot about the car, about Jamshed.

"How do you feel?" he said, after what must have been a very long time.

"Alright."

"You'll feel happy in a little while."

*

Before the start of the following year, I was expelled.

I tried. I stayed up nights on end staring at the pages of my textbooks. In the early hours, while the city slept and silence loomed on the streets, I sat still and bleary-eyed at my desk, hunched over *Foundations of Physics*, *General Chemistry*, and *Fundamentals of Calculus*. But as the weeks progressed, during the temperate winter nights when the papers on my desk fluttered in the cool sea breeze through the windows, I began to hear things. Night after night, muted at first, then loud, I heard things. Thump. Thump. Thump. Slow and quiet, thump, thump, thump, at first.

I tried to read. I opened a book I enjoyed, like *David Copperfield*, and tried to read.

Thump, thump, thump.

I drew my face into the book, my face inches from the page, and tried to read.

Thump, thump, thump. Thump, thump, thud. Thump, thud, thud. Like a pounding hammer, thud, thud, thud.

I walked across the hall to my brother's room and switched on the light.

He was fast asleep. I switched off the light and returned to my room.

I sat again at my desk and tried to read.

Thump, thump, thump.

I plugged my earphones into the radio and listened—to anything.

Thump, thump, thump.

I turned up the volume.

Thud, thud, thud.

I switched from station to station, flipped page after page.

Thud, thud, thud.

I stood up and sat down, stood up and sat down.

Thud, thud, thud.

I walked across again to my brother's room. But he was soundly asleep.

I returned to my desk and switched off the lights.

Thud, thud, thud.

I climbed into bed and lay on my stomach.

Thud, thud, thud.

I pushed my face into the mattress, pulled the pillow over my head.

Thud, thud, thud.

I sat up, sweating.

Thud.

Thud.

Thud.

I ran across the hall, jumped on my brother's mattress, grabbed his head, and held it down into the pillow.

He usually woke up, startled.

I lay on the floor beside his bed until he fell asleep.

Then I drank a shot of scotch or brandy from the bar in the living room.

The sounds in my head slowly faded, and I, too, fell asleep.

*

I'm almost eighteen.

I help my father with the business. Sometimes I manage it alone. Often, I drive a van around the city to pick up new merchandise from railway stations, from the breweries, and, in the far-flung suburbs, from unlicensed distilleries concealed in tall, smelly marshes on the fringe of the land, along isolated parts of the coast, or deep in the slums.

Business is good. Tomorrow night a large shipment will arrive from Mombasa on a cargo vessel. It'll then journey some way in a trawler; then, fishermen will bring the crates to the shore in canoes, lanterns flickering like fireflies in the smog.

I'll be waiting on the beach with the van.

Jamshed and I have never lost touch. We used to meet every week, at least once. He'd accompany me to work some weekends or, with friends, join me later. We'd take a suite upstairs overlooking the sea and stay up all night, talking, gambling, smoking, drinking.

If I'd never come to know him, I would have clung to school. I used to think it was the only path. But he helped me see things clearly. I'll never know why he, so popular, took to me. But I think he was ahead of his years: already, at fifteen, he had tired of the others, outgrown them. They sought him out the way their parents sought out his parents, but they bored him. He saw their predictable futures, like those of their fathers, executives at multinational corporations, members of mercantile organizations, of private clubs. He saw them in suits and ties, in carpeted, curtained plush offices, in teak-furnished boardrooms. Their lives, an extension of their lives as students, would not be so different from his own father's. But it was a future that terrified him, a future, now that he is cured, secure for him.

The admiral still runs the school. I heard he said that Jamshed, traveling around the world, was a model student, an example that all young New Cantuarians should aspire to. But everyone knew Jamshed was only in one place: on a beautiful lakeside campus with gardens and trees not far from Lausanne, rehabilitating. He's back now and will rejoin school next year, and finish it. Then he'll go to college.

In a way, we're perfect complements. Each day after I left school, I drifted farther and farther from my past, as he moved closer and closer to that world despite being a rebel, despite so much hashish, so much opium, until his parents noticed, until the doctor told them, your son's a junkie. I knew I wanted to be a psychiatrist when I was young. I'll probably never become that. Jamshed knew what he didn't ever want to be, and will become that.

I saw him just yesterday. He hadn't been to the store in months, having been in Switzerland, and offered to drive me to work. Later we would be joined by friends, some from school and some, older, from Saint Sebastian.

On our way, while we waited at a red light at the busy intersection at Kemps Corner, a girl, about five or six, with tattered, dirty clothes—one of the city's countless beggars—stood outside my window on her toes and strained her neck to peep inside. She extended me her palm. I pulled out my wallet, lowered the window, gave her two rupees, and raised the window.

"What's the matter with you?" said Jamshed.

"What?"

"Nothing. Look…"

The girl still stood there, her other palm extended.

I reached again for my wallet.

"Fuck," he said, "what's the matter with you? How can you let people take advantage of you like this?"

The lights were changing and Jamshed shifted into first. To the left and right the cars were crawling forward, and from behind they honked.

"Wait," I said.

The lights changed. My eyes met the girl's as the window lowered. She raised her hand farther as Jamshed pressed on the pedal. Then I felt a gust of wind as off we went, and she, with her empty palm, disappeared.

MEIN BRUDER?

I stayed two nights in Amsterdam, then rented a car and drove east. It was June. The road was straight. It cut through the fields that turned lime when the clouds shifted, saturated with light, the luminosity the Old Masters loved.

I sped up on the Autobahn, the stray windmills behind me, the road monotonous for two hours, the radio stations, Dutch, German, English, fading in and out. Ahead were commerce and industry, office buildings and factories, billboards with logos of car and chemical companies rising on both sides.

On the stretch to Bonn, the great Cologne cathedral, Gothic, brown, sad, crept into the rearview mirror and dissolved into the overarching soft blue. I was ascending. Long-abandoned castles loomed on the hills. The Rhine flashed between trees, trailing me to the pier across the Arp Museum, where I waited for the ferry to cross the river.

I was entering a foreign interior, its sleepy, provincial hamlets, their cobblestone streets with the family bakery, the chocolatier, unspoiled by tourists. I drove through a town with a crumbling medieval church and wooden loam-and-straw-insulated houses, up a narrow winding two-lane road flanked by a forest, to the top of the slope.

A lanky man in aviator sunglasses holding a cellphone sat on a folding chair beside a car outside his gate. "Welcome," he said, extending his hand as I stepped out. "I am Bernhard. Gabriele asked me to wait here ready. She was sure you would get lost."

I heard my name called out, the unmistakable voice, the inflection. She ran down the porch toward us. Her hair had turned gray, but otherwise it was how I remembered it, full and wavy. I had forgotten how tall she was, how long her legs were.

The past surged over me, the rendezvous in European cities, the days spent in conversation in cafés, Tabula Rasa, Sehnsucht, Pavlov, and, back home, the long-distance phone chats that ended at dawn in Boston.

Bernhard beamed as we embraced. He brought the cars into the driveway while she and I went inside, arms around each other's waists.

*

"How many years?" said Gabriele. "Eighteen?"

"More than twenty."

The silence between us of two decades was lifting, a silence that had begun in the mid-nineteen-nineties, just months after we first met, and had only recently been breached by a postcard I sent on an impulse to an old address that had been forwarded to her.

"*Ja*, maybe something like that."

She looked thoughtful. She was slicing bread. An assortment of cheeses lay on a cutting board. On the table were bottles of oil, a Riesling, in the center a thin vase with a tulip, dishes with a salad, Brussels sprouts, a honey-glazed chicken.

"I am sorry my English is not so good."

"It's fine."

"No, it is not. You will correct me, no? Please. How else will I learn? Bernhard too."

"It's really fine. It's better than you think."

"Will you have some salad?"

"*Sa*lad."

"*Was*?" She giggled and covered her mouth. "What?"

"Salad. Not sa*lad*."

"Ah."

At the other end of the room, past a sofa and a coffee table, was a Knauss Coblenz, a minuet transcription propped up on the music rack, and behind the piano, against the wall, was a sideboard with a bouquet and a double picture frame with a photograph of her mother on the left, her father on the right.

The patio doors were open, the air was warm and still. The back of the house faced the woods, a grand linden visible through the kitchen windows past the garden, Norwegian spruces beyond. Off parts of the gravel trails that ran for miles were parallel ruts with impressions of wheels of ancient Roman carts once used to transport precious metals. Collectibles had been excavated there as recently as a hundred years ago. Bernhard had a book about them. He stood up to get it.

"I think—you are an historian—you will like it," he said, handing it to me.

"I'm not a numismatist."

He sat down again. There was silence.

"I'm not," I said, "an expert on coins."

"Yes, politics is your specialization."

"Political history."

They had talked about me. They looked too close to each other not to have, immersed in the acquiescence that came from more than ten good years together, from wedlock, from pasts, still unraveling, that had ushered them separately to this quiet suburban existence. It seemed strange and yet explicable that the two had once lived for years on the same street, directly across from each other, in Düsseldorf, that years later they had both traveled to Nice, visited the same vineyards, enjoyed the same wines, the summer before they met.

He knew we had had a correspondence before the days of the Internet and email, a flurry of handwritten letters wrapped around photos, sealed in envelopes, dispatched with stamps. She had saved everything. He knew I was then a lecturer at Emerson College. He knew I had visited her in Cologne, where she then lived, a strapped, single mother studying nursing at night after graduating from a philosophy program at a university.

"How many times?" I asked.

"Three," she said. "I think."

"I thought two."

"No, I think more. Maybe four."

"How is your research?" said Bernhard.

I was working on a book on the 1947 Partition of India to be published in four years, in 2022, simultaneously in India, in the US, and in translation in Germany. Sifting through private documents and personal accounts, news articles and printed propaganda, I was consumed by the process of interpreting and narrating one of the greatest atrocities of the previous century, the barbaric end of a barbaric occupation that left a nation fractured, two million dead, and twenty million displaced.

The project had become a puzzle: each new piece of information was corroborating some loose association between ostensibly unrelated things; events, lives, fates were becoming entangled, cohering into a whole that straddled continents. There were interviews with survivors and their descendants, some of them, as I uncovered, distant relatives in Asia, in Europe, in the Americas. The book had become so personal I was ill at ease speaking about it at forums.

Felix Biesinger, after one such event at Princeton, walked up to me and handed me his card. "I know your father's work," he said. "I admire it. I even met him once."

I had never heard of him, but learned he published up to four titles a year, and in some years none. He stalked his subjects—on the current list were the Herero and Namaqua genocide, the Union Carbide disaster, the Chagossian expulsion—like a prosecutor preparing for a high-profile case. A settlement, however, was not an option in the face of fact. When he took on something, he did so intent on setting the historical record straight.

Then he executed by proxy, soliciting the right author for the thesis at hand.

He had fended off some dozen lawsuits, from corporations, from foundations, two from governments. At his office on Harvard Square, where I went to sign the contract, he quoted a passage from *Faust*, then asked for my personal cellphone number. I was to keep it on at all hours for the duration of our agreement. "Clause 4c," he said, "and it's not in fine print." He had ideas sometimes in the middle of the night, seminal but fleeting ideas, and at those moments he needed to be able to contact an author immediately.

"I'm on sabbatical. I'm frequently not in the States. I don't have roaming."

"Get it," he said, handing me a check.

Since then, I had started traveling back and forth from Boston to Calcutta regularly, as much as four times a year, occasionally stopping in Europe to meet him.

"You should come here more often now," said Gabriele.

*

I had had dinner with Felix in Amsterdam the previous night at De Yjsbreker. It was capacious and chic. Gone was the bohemian interior I remembered, the dim lighting and the oak tables by the tall windows where, more than twenty years ago, I had sat with Gabriele. At night we had walked across the city to the hotel, she holding my arm, the canals gleaming.

The book was sure to lose money, the research barely supported by grants. But Felix didn't care. He was proud of his autonomy, his legacy. He was the great-grandson of the cofounder of Biesinger-Wiegand Verlag. His grandfather had bought out the partner. His father, who had built an art collection that was rumored to be priceless, had led an underground cell that had disrupted meetings of the National Socialists.

Outside his headquarters in Munich, Felix had offices, modestly staffed, but offices nevertheless, in Johannesburg, Buenos Aires, and Boston. At trade shows, word would get around quickly if he was present. Most of his peers feared him, some befriended him; all envied him.

He was devoted to his authors, as he was to his wife of forty years. They were in transit, on their way to Ireland. He was wearing white khakis, a striped lime-and-mustard shirt, a pink jacket, a Panama hat. The sun was a platinum sheet skimming the canal, the glare unrelenting. They had been walking all day, dodging bicycles.

"Why didn't you tell me before you were going to Germany?" he asked.

The sidewalk café was busy. The tablecloth, beige with lace borders, had circles from the rims of our glasses.

"It was impromptu," I said.

"Too bad. Maybe Anna and I would have postponed our trip and had you over. And your translator."

His eyes were wandering like a scoundrel's.

"Churchill," he said loudly, "was the biggest mother-fucker of the twentieth century." He sipped his prosecco.

There were tourists, delegates of an international conference at the Amstel Hotel across the bridge. Some still had their badges on, like Nigel Pickering and his colleagues, all talking with the same accent, at the table to my left. He had brought a spoon to his mouth, then stopped to glance at Felix, who, as if awaiting the moment, peered over his shades, and said, "Churchill, your national hero. The great war criminal."

People were looking, or looking away. Anna sighed, leaned back, and lit a cigarette. "Felix thinks he's the Klaus Kinski of publishing," she said.

He rested his cigar in the ashtray, placed his hands over his belly, gazed at the sun, and laughed. "Klaus was the Felix of film."

"And I'm more beautiful than Nastassja."

"Did you know I wanted to do a book on Klaus when he was alive?"

"What happened?" I asked.

"I couldn't find anyone to write it. Everyone was afraid of him."

"Ha!"

"I even wanted to do a book on Mother Theresa."

"And?"

"She wouldn't cooperate. I've learned it's easier to revive the dead in books than to enshrine the living."

His stogie had gone out. He tapped the ash off the tip, brought it to his mouth, lit it, and clenched it between his teeth. "Who are you staying with in Bonn? A girlfriend I don't know about?"

"No."

"Who?"

"An old friend."

"Bullshit."

*

The project had its origins in work my father had begun at the University of Calcutta, where he had his first job. He loved it, the city that bred him, home. He taught three days a week, spent Sundays drinking rum and playing bridge at the Bengal Club. He lived in a family bungalow with a thirty-foot-long verandah and fifteen-foot ceilings.

But nothing, other than a paper published in a little-known journal, ever came of his early research. By the time he had begun to receive invitations from American colleges, his interests had shifted to areas away from revisionist history, to anthropology, to archeology, even to art, especially prehistoric art, the relics of antiquity. They were, he once said in a lecture holding up reproductions of two headless statuettes, the silent stalwarts of heritage, the ambassadors of time; they testified to all that was admirable about the human condition, all that was deplorable about it.

During the days, while Bernhard and Gabriele were at work, I sat on the porch and edited my drafts, sifted through interview transcripts, logged into library accounts and read.

Evenings we talked in the living room, a red fin-de-siècle chandelier from a Viennese thrift shop above, candles on the mantel. She had the day shift at a regional hospital. He was a chemical engineer at a food processing plant.

"I would never eat anything we manufacture," he said.

They had met in the waiting room of a psychotherapist. At middle age, after his father's death, his failed first marriage, he had decided his faith, which he had never questioned, had been leading him to an abyss. His study was lined with books on Eastern occult, Buddhism, ancient pagan practices. He would read an hour each night while she played the piano.

"You're very lucky to have each other," I said.

"Really?" She was straightening the curls in her hair with her fingers. She smiled.

"Hmm," she said. "I think we are both very lucky to have this house. We would never get a bank loan separately. Right, my dear Bernhard?"

Outspoken and expressive, she was his opposite. She liked exploring the mysteries of the makers coded in great paintings and sculptures, in great poems, that revealed themselves slowly. In the bookcases outside their room upstairs were collections of Tsvetaeva, Bachmann, biographies of Michelangelo, van Gogh, Klee, Rothko.

"What did you do today?" she asked.

"Work," I said.

"You're working very hard. Tomorrow we will all go out."

Saturday, we went for a hike in the morning, on a trail that led to a stone chapel in a clearing, then drove to the farmer's market outside Bonn, then to the city.

"Why are the ceilings so low?" I said at Beethoven-Haus. We were stooping.

"The Germans were very small people then," she said.

"Like the Borrowers," I said.

"Like what?"

"The Borrowers, the tiny people." I held my thumb and forefinger an inch apart. "They're this big. There's a book about them."

They laughed.

"Maybe a children's book," she said.

At home, there were three messages in German on the answering machine.

"So," said Gabriele, "it is confirmed."

"What?"

"A surprise. My sisters are coming for dinner tomorrow. They want to meet you. And Anton will also come from Cologne."

*

"Our mother was a very weak woman," said Ute. "This is why no man stayed with her." She was seated to my left. She was the eldest, built like a diva.

"She doesn't look that way in the photo," I said.

"That is a pose," she said. "You do not know. She fell in love too easily. Always with the wrong man."

She leaned toward me, held two fingers in front of my face, and wiggled them. "She had two bad marriages," she said. "What more can I say?"

"It is true," said Astrid, leaning over, her palms on the table. She had brought in the pasta from the kitchen. She sat down opposite me. "She could not find a proper husband for herself, a proper father for her daughters."

"Not one of us knew our father," said Ute. "*I* had to take care of both the girls."

"I wish sometimes I had a brother," said Astrid.

"What a nice thing to say in front of Gabi and me."

"I did not mean it like that."

"No? Well, I wish *I* had a brother. So there."

"Ladies," said Hans. "We have a guest." He was reading the new *Du*, he did not look up.

"She was very needy. That was her one big mistake in life."

"Please do not say things like that about our mother. Are you not needy? Hans, you tell us: is Ute needy or not?"

"Be quiet," said Ute. "Hans is the needy one." She took a sip of her wine and looked straight ahead at nothing in particular. "Why did you abandon Gabi?"

I stirred the ice in my glass with a finger. "I didn't abandon her," I said. "I'm here."

She turned to me. "It is like you disappeared with the millennium."

"I got a full-time job," I said, "a professorship. There were committee meetings, administration, teaching, grading, research."

"*Ja, ja, ja.*" She looked straight ahead again. "Is it because of your father?"

"What do you mean?"

"I heard he published many books."

"Yes. He was ambitious. He worked hard. He won awards. He was liked and respected. It's hard to fill his shoes."

"Did he not allow you to meet Gabi?"

I ran my thumb along a crease in the tablecloth.

"It wasn't that," I said.

"So you get a job and disappear, *whoosh*, like the wind?"

"It's complicated."

"How, exactly, 'complicated'?"

"His health was not good."

"You did not reply her letters even. Gabi was—what is the word?"

"Unsatisfied," said Gabriele. She was standing at the table, oven mitts on, hands on hips.

"Yes, unsatisfied," said Ute. "Especially after she found you and then lost you."

"Let it be," said Gabriele.

I poured myself another jigger of whiskey.

"As I remember it," I said, "I found her."

"She was sad, more than sad. She was—what is the word?"

"Distraught?"

"What means that?" She clapped her hands. "Somebody, bring the dictionary. Hans, bring me the dictionary. It is behind your head."

Bernhard came in from the kitchen, placed the salad on the table, kissed Gabriele, and went back.

"Now we are having English lessons," said Anton from the sofa, a laptop on his knees. "This is boring. I need more wine."

"Come and get it yourself," said Astrid.

Ute nudged me. "How do you spell it?" She had the dictionary sliced open with her hand.

"Spell what?"

"That word you just said."

"Distraught. D, i…"

"Work, work, work. That is all Americans do," said Astrid.

"That's not true."

"Why are you still single then?"

Ute shut the dictionary and pushed it aside. "Astrid had an American boyfriend once upon a time," she said. "It was a disaster."

"Why?"

"Someone was too needy," she said, chuckling.

"Not me," said Astrid.

"Why are *you* still single then?"

"Ladies," said Hans.

"You must see the Cologne cathedral," said Anton, filling his glass behind Astrid.

"I have," I said.

"No. You must go up."

"I have."

"When?"

"Exactly, let me see, twenty-one years ago, with you and your mother."

"No!"

"Yes."

"How I do not remember?"

"You were a little boy," said Gabriele.

A Janáček string quartet was playing on the stereo. Gabriele lowered the volume and turned on the chandelier.

My phone rang.

It was Felix. "Do you have time?" he said.

I walked to the porch and down to the garden. The trees were becoming silhouettes, the lights in neighboring houses were turning on. The white half-moon hovered above a roof.

"Do you know the films of Aantya Huq?"

"I know the name. She was a political something. My dad, I remember, had videotapes."

"They've been digitally remastered. I have the boxed set, just released from a publisher in Hamburg; it has subtitles in four languages. I've brought them here. I've been watching them."

"How are they?"

"Splendid. There are very revealing interviews with her on one DVD. She's opened a world unknown to me, a short-lived mid-century avant-garde theater and cinema movement related to your subject."

"Interesting."

"I'd like you to do a chapter on performing arts and film."

"I'm not sure…"

"She'd be a good place to start. I've arranged for you to meet her later this month. She's a recluse, lives outside Calcutta. Her husband was briefly your father's colleague. He wrote the obituary for him in *The Economist*."

"I didn't know."

"In one old interview, she attributes her inspiration to an obscure academic paper." He paused. "Your dad's, it turns out."

"Incredible."

"They had an affair as well, but that's not relevant."

It had rained in the afternoon. The leaves on the linden were glistening.

"He was a bachelor then," I said.

I felt the breeze on my cheeks as I went back inside.

Someone had shut the patio doors; someone had brought an extra chair from upstairs. The food had been laid out. Everyone was seated and talking.

"See what I said?" said Astrid. "Work, work, work."

"It was a German who called," I said.

Bernhard laughed, stood up, and walked around the table with the salad. He placed some in all the plates but one: he forgot mine.

Gabriele noticed.

"*Und mein Bruder?*" she said.

"Sorry," he said.

I looked up at her, but she didn't see me. She was passing the tray of sausages across the table to Hans.

Bernhard came over and I held out my plate. As I put it down, Gabriele's eyes met mine.

I looked away.

"What is the matter?" she said.

"Nothing," I said, reaching for the bread. "It's 'meine

Bruder,' isn't it?"

"I see you are learning German," said Ute.

"No," said Gabriele, "it is masculine and singular, 'mein *Bruder.*'"

I looked up at her again. She was focused on the parmesan cheese she was grating over her plate, attentive to the thin flakes as they curled and fell on the salad.

Bernhard sat down. *"Guten appetit,"* he said.

I heard the clink of silverware on china as I looked over Gabriele's shoulder to the sideboard behind the piano, to the amaryllises she had brought in that afternoon from the garden, to the photographs of her parents: her long-suffering mother, the Teutonic face stern in profile; her father, whose eyes she had, whom she had met when he visited Berlin on the pretext of a conference after she tracked him down and wrote him—she was twenty-five then—a letter that began, "I am your daughter, who you have never seen…"

Her father, our father, the Ivy League professor, now dead, who spent his mid-twenties in Bavaria, a paying guest at her mother's; who after his postdoc bought a Volkswagen convertible he drove through Europe and then shipped to Calcutta—the only one in the city, he used to say—papa, not only brilliant but also dashing, who kept a secret from his wife, my mother, and from his son until it was too late, until he received a letter that, as he said in confidence to me, shook his foundations, after which his health deteriorated so much that, barely sixty and looking like an old man, he never really recovered.

PSALM

1

The first Monday in October, Joel Bernstein didn't show up for work.

I stood in the conference room by the cold, glass wall. Below, streetlamps lit the promenades in Central Park, a rectangular swath hazy in mist, the leaves yet to turn. Along the avenues, signals changed, and every now and then a car flashed by. Crisp and autumnal, moonlight brushed the city. In a few hours its rank and file would meld into the vortex of rush hour, surge through the capillaries of subway trains and high-rise elevators. But for now, they slept.

The partners, the analysts, the traders ambled in. The smell of coffee was strong. White Styrofoam cups sat beside dossiers on the granite tabletop. Someone brewed another pot.

"So where is he?"

Everyone had taken their places.

The question had been directed at me, but I didn't know the answer. I walked to the head of the table.

"Didn't he call you? Text you?"

He hadn't. But it was understood during the ensuing silence that the meeting would take place, and that I would lead it. More than five years ago, after a fiscal quarter in which I oversaw a sequence of trades more lucrative for Panorama Capital than all the trades the preceding two years combined, Bernstein had insisted I sit in the front.

"I got lucky," I'd said.

"Nonsense," Bernstein had said, "you're being modest."

On the one hand, everything in finance happened predictably; on the other hand, nothing did. I was responsible for teasing out uncertainties in investments without suffocating the firm with insurance costs or exposing it to excessive risk while ensuring a healthy profit. In other words, I was responsible, at least informally, for more or less what everyone did. If it weren't for the whims of the markets, the nights that kept me sleepless, I might have believed Bernstein: I didn't just get lucky, especially when, outdoing myself within a year, I made him a Wall Street darling and his firm one of the most vaunted hedge funds.

"I got lucky again."

"Nonsense," scoffed Bernstein. The office across from his had never been occupied. "You're moving in there today. Now get lost."

I sat down, thumbed the sheaf of papers before me, ill at ease with the void to my left. Bernstein would have reclined, hands behind his head, and squinted at the blinking smoke detector on the ceiling, as if deciphering an oracle—maybe about the relationship between Mother's Day and the value of the Turkish lira—and, before turning to everyone else, have looked at me and said, "What do you think?"

Half the people in the room didn't mind me; some regarded me with respect, if not awe. The other half hid their contempt, if not their envy.

"What's up with Japan?" I began.

During the next two hours, mutual ambition and camaraderie, the challenge of collectively decrypting the cryptic—of structuring a trade beyond any competitor's comprehension—overtook the awkwardness and tediousness, the shrugging and the doodling. Cuffs were unbuttoned, sleeves rolled up, hairdos mussed, coffee spilled, newspaper clippings and bulletins soiled with butter and donut stains. We felt like a dozen or so would-be demigods as, dawn approaching, we contemplated the world as an abstraction, taking the hemispheres in our stride, traversing time zones from east to west, homing in on the major countries, the minor ones. We spewed out facts and rumors, exchange rates, interest rates, indexes; the projections, the policies; the political trends and uncertainties; who said what in the news, who posted what on which blog. The shy PhD from Stanford weighed in, the cocksure MBA from Columbia. We outlined scenarios, crushed paper plates and brown bags from ordered-in breakfasts. *What would Joel think?* someone said. Someone else, *Joel would love that*, or *Joel would never go for that.*

A new chairman, more hawkish than the retiring one, was being sworn in at the National Bank of Korea: maybe there was a short-term window of opportunity there just before the press conference. The yield curve in Indonesia was showing signs of inversion: maybe the region mandated a closer look. Euphoria after the election of a new government in Nigeria that promised an end to corrupt corporate practices had caused its stock market to rally fifty percent in one week, buoyed by European funds; but notably, Germany had stayed out, following government proceedings against E. K. Wolf, an industrial conglomerate, on charges of bribery in neighboring Niger.

By nine it was clear we would prolong a small position we had taken the previous week in a recently privatized steel plant in the Czech Republic. It had so far made us a paper profit of sixty percent, or sixty million dollars. There were no signs of the euro becoming volatile. It was clear that two IPOs scheduled on American exchanges for the week could not be ignored, one of a Chinese airline, one of a European telecom.

The frost had melted. Sunlight drenched the park. The staff trickled in. A few phone calls later we had ironed out the details of a complex, leveraged trade with speculative positions on the euro and the yuan. We would exit in two weeks with a tidy eight-figure profit, maybe nine, days before a crucial domestic Federal Reserve meeting, which no doubt would rattle the markets.

All that was needed was Bernstein's approval.

*

Bernstein's approval never came.

He didn't show up that day or the rest of the week. He didn't call, he couldn't be reached. Tuesday, we became restless. The exchange rates scrolling across our terminals started to drive home the cost of our missed opportunity. Each minute deflated our imagined bonuses. Each hour led to compounding disappointment.

On Wednesday the euro plunged after a terrorist attack in Rome. There were two dozen casualties. A fringe Marxist group, Commitalia, took responsibility. It claimed it had cells in every country in the Eurozone, and it promised more attacks in undisclosed capitals, even at ports of trading partners as far as Asia. Separately, EKW was likely to be fined billions; the bribes were linked to an accident at a small African bauxite mine that had caused more than twenty deaths two months before. It had been covered up— until now. Had the trade been approved, by afternoon Panorama would have been eight hundred million dollars in the red; each minute it held its position, its losses would have multiplied. By Thursday it would have had margin calls it could not meet, and within hours would have been wiped out, reduced to a week of headlines, a decade of lawsuits, and a textbook case study for finance majors.

Luck, I learned, was one side of a coin called irony.

2

Bernstein's scheduled appearance on Thursday afternoon on TV had to be canceled. "Call EFBC and tell them it has to be rescheduled," I told the office assistant.

Friday evening, I sat in my car, windows lowered, on the north side of East Eighty-Seventh Street, a few doors west of the building on the opposite side in which Bernstein lived. The sky was tinged apricot. To my right was the non-descript, concrete wall of a residential co-op. Evergreens rose along it from a stretch of grass behind a balustrade that turned on the sidewalk to Fifth Avenue. At the edge of the curb were tree pits with colorful pansies, cornucopias of poker faces. Joggers, cyclists whizzed past; people walked in and out of the park, the museums.

I watched the entrance, glass doors below a burgundy awning, from the rearview mirror, the taxis that pulled over, who entered, who left. I called. The same message played on Bernstein's cellphone that had played all week.

I listened to the radio. WNYC, Q104.3, Bloomberg, switching stations back and forth. Lights changed at the intersection ahead—WALK, DON'T WALK—and the SUV at the front of the block reflected red, green, red, green. I slumped, sat up, slumped again. I peed on the curb when it was clear. I had Mimi's on Lexington Avenue deliver pizza to the car.

It was dark. I peered out to see if the penthouse lights

were on.

At midnight, I drove home down a trafficless FDR.

*

I'd been upstairs at Bernstein's only once, at the holiday party my first year at Panorama, the last year he hosted it there. The living room was recessed from the vestibule. The tall exposures faced south, the Chrysler Building rising on the left, Hell's Kitchen and the theater district lit up below on the right.

Winter. The trees leafless. The metropolis at once stripped and decked for December. Bernstein's view when he read Ibsen and Strindberg, the wide stretch of sky, city blocks beneath like a stage backdrop.

He was on the board of the New York Academy of Theater Arts, and raffled tickets at the office for orchestra seats. Off the dining room was a compact library, walls lined with walnut bookcases with first editions of Eugene O'Neill, Arthur Miller, Tennessee Williams, rare signed or transcribed copies in Mylar jackets.

The next time I dined with him was a few years later, when he invited me, following my successes, to Benford's for dinner, midweek in August. I'd never heard of it, looked up the address, and at six hopped in a cab in the sweltering heat and headed to the West Village, shirt untucked, tie loose, jacket still draped over my chair at the office.

I was late. Bernstein, unruffled in a linen suit, was waiting in the foyer and walked up as the concierge was about to say something. "You're not going to put my son through that, are you?"

"House rules, sir." He meant the jacket. "Sorry. What's your size?" I was tucking in my shirt, straightening my tie.

52

"I'll bring one to you."

Inside, a fat bald man in a red velvet blazer was playing the piano. We sat at a table at the back of the large hall, off the fireplace, by a window that overlooked Commerce Street.

The wine came, the hors d'oeuvres; but not the jacket. The maître d', the waiters, everyone knew him, called him Joel. He insisted on that. Sometimes he asked them to pick his courses, told them he had too much on his mind to think about food.

"He must have believed me when I said you're my son." He leaned back in his chair, clasped his hands behind his head. He looked up at the ceiling. He squinted. "The statistical odds of it," he said, "aren't bad. Half the men in this business, more or less, are Jews; the other half, more or less, are Indians."

We laughed.

"'The best choose one thing above all,' Heraclitus said," said Bernstein, "'the everlasting fame of mortals.' I'm not sure. Fame fades, and even if it has an afterlife, both fame and mortals are capricious. Money, on the other hand, can make for an even-keeled journey through the ravaging storm that's life."

I looked at him, perplexed by what he said, by how he said it, by how, for an instant, he was a person different than the one I knew at the office. He noticed. "As long as you're not one of the wannabe Gatsbys, a dime a dozen, going down with his yacht when the tailwinds stop blowing.

"But if it weren't for them, we'd have fewer good clients. God bless them."

I could not tell with his dismissiveness whether he was being derisive or affectionate. He wore both, derision and affection, like a bespoke ensemble. When he weighed in on something, his hands did most of the work without moving much, and it was impossible to pinpoint—as he recounted facts in a considered, assured, and avuncular way—what exactly he was thinking.

This held up well on TV. He calmed investors on turbulent days, elicited laughter. Each appearance guaranteed one or two substantial fund transfers to Panorama.

He raised his hand, his forefinger. "Do you know what this is? It's a piano transcription of Lutosławski's second symphony. It's being performed next weekend at Carnegie Hall."

I saw how he could, with a comment, deflect attention away from himself, his inmost convictions, then fling the crux of the conversation farther, off-limits, with a gesture. Even as he drew attention to himself, he diverted it away, made it, with the turn of a phrase, ricochet elsewhere. He would remain inscrutable. When he seemed intimate, he was whittling you into confession. He was breaking you in, slowly but surely.

We talked about the new hires, their performances, the kid who had written a touching personal letter to Bernstein—"my hero"—about his family, his father's drinking, his sister's autism, his mother's desperation; about how he, doing odd jobs at bodegas, was working through a business degree at Bronx Community College; about how much he wanted to do something with his life.

Bernstein had him called in. He gave him an internship.

"His translations into Spanish of our newsletters and the transcripts of your talks are attracting a lot of attention to our website," I said. "We'll have a bilingual online presence by the end of the summer. No other firm has that."

The Friday before Memorial Day, Bernstein had called everyone to the conference room. Two interns would begin the following week, he said. The staff could use them for photocopying, answering the phones, whatever. But if anyone felt compelled to condescend to either of them, they would condescend to "the other kid," the junior from Dartmouth. No one would condescend to Oscar.

Or else.

The light from the chandelier fell unevenly across Bernstein's face as he sat back, made of it a lambent mosaic. He appeared like a stained-glass depiction of himself, which was not so unlike how he was perceived, pieced together, by those who ostensibly knew him, as a puzzle formed from brief conversations, from glimpses of him on EFBC, or at an opera or a gala. Seldom did anyone who worked for him see him or hear from him after he left the office at six and before he arrived at seven, though on Mondays he was often there even before I was.

"I met Betty online," he said, "on an upscale site that charges ninety-nine bucks a month. As good, but cheaper, than the shadchan I've used for years."

Who was Betty?

"Any plans to settle down?"

"Not yet."

"I should introduce you to Betty's daughter."

Bernstein opened his satchel and pulled out a wooden box of Dominican Cohibas. He placed it on the table. "Take it," he said, "you'll enjoy them. Oscar brought them from his trip home last week to meet his grandmother. But I don't smoke."

*

Saturday morning, before 5 AM, I drove back.

I double-parked in the middle of Bernstein's block.

55

Lights from lobbies splashed on the sidewalks.

I was sipping hot coffee I'd picked up from an all-night deli on Second Avenue when I sensed movement. From between the shadows, a woman, first a silhouette, appeared. She wore a black skirt, black stockings, a black leather overcoat she held clasped at the collar. She approached in the dark, mysterious and beautiful. At the car in front of mine, she fumbled in her purse for keys, half her face aglow from the streetlight. Her lips were full, her cheekbones high, her profile slim. Like a model in a glossy magazine, she wore no emotion. The surrounding apartments were in the thousands, apartments disused, apartments lived-in and furnished, walls with Picassos and Mirós, stone balconies like loges, calico and velvet curtains sweeping across exposures. Apartments reached by carpeted winding, marble stairs with polished, hardwood banisters, by birdcage elevators. What mattered was, she emerged, not from where. The night had fed her, the night had starved her: I would never know. But at that moment, she was mine. Looking into her rearview mirror, she straightened her bangs. Then she drove off.

Lust turned to loneliness as I moved into the empty spot. I promised myself I'd never leave, I'd die in the city. The disappointments it rendered at its most inert, most somnam-bulant, were alive and palpable. They spurred dreams and hope, spawned fantasy.

At any rate, I was too far along to change course. Bernstein had all but taken care of that. How far the city had receded that once felt like a one-way street converging to a point beyond which, as in a painting, was nothing, toward which each day nudged me. How the firsts had faded: first job, first colleague, Delta, Angus. What had happened of them? Angus and I, just days apart in age, at the table in the small meeting room off the pantry, reviewing brochures, exotic derivatives being marketed to Delta Advantage.

"I see what's going on here," I had said.

"You do?"

I had sketched out the scenarios. Later, after work, we had gone to Papi's for dinner, where the elegant crowd talked in whispers. We had resumed our conversation from the afternoon.

"I still don't get it."

He'd managed to scrape through a degree in economics from Georgetown, could not make head or tail of the securities. But he needed to discuss them with clients in sufficient detail, with authority, with slides projected on a whiteboard, a laser pointer in hand, to have intricacies distilled into plain English. He had to sound good, but not too good.

I'd wanted his job, the better of the two jobs posted.

"We're positioning you for the other opening," the recruiter said to me.

Why not the job for which I'd applied?

"We've sent in someone else for that. He's just too super right for it."

I said nothing. The recruiter adjusted his tie. At his side was a trainee. Her straight hair ran behind her ears and curled over her nape. She wore a platinum band around the neck.

"He's moved in the right circles, you know?" she said. "He moves easily among them."

I said nothing. She shrugged.

"He looks great in a double-breasted suit," said the recruiter, in the manner of a joke. "It's what they want."

I said nothing. He looked at her.

"His father's a congressman," she said.

A few days a week, Angus scuttled in and out of the Yale Club, the University Club. I, on the other hand, didn't own a double-breasted suit. I didn't have a congressman father.

I did not, as far back as I could remember, have a father.

Word had it he had been poisoned. He was the marketing manager at a chemicals manufacturer, where he had moved three rungs up in seniority in two consecutive years. He had accounts all over the country, was starting initiatives for expansion in Malaysia, in Scandinavia. He hosted quarterly parties at the New Delhi Gibson Club—where his boss was a member—following two days of meetings. He could talk all day, then talk all night, hold his scotch and gin. Colleagues his junior—more than twice his age, employed four times as long as he—patted his back and brought him drinks as he mingled. Attachés of foreign trade offices called him weekly, invited him to diplomatic luncheons.

One evening, while a corporate event's reception was still underway, his assistant drove him home. He was staggering, had to be propped up. He died that night. I was two. A month later, my mother had a miscarriage.

The years that followed—promising years for enterprising men and women—marked the beginning of economic liberalization in India following decades of protectionism, of a forthcoming surge in international trade, of Japanese and German cars on local roads, of Coca-Cola and Pepsi billboards. Change resonated everywhere, not just at meetings of Chambers of Commerce, which, when I was older, I learned my classmates' fathers attended, but also on the streets, where vendors sold flowers, newspapers, candy floss. Even the cab drivers had started to speak in English.

What could in a social gathering relish more than the narrative of a family's emergence out of the lower middle class at an opportune moment, its plunge again into despair by misfortune while everyone else prospered? As my mother saw me through the Connaught Place Academy, privately tutoring students my age for money, a venom was slowly and steadily working through me. It was poisoning my youth, the city, its people, the biannual open house weekends when, in sunshine, the school lawn bustled with parents, men in khakis and blue blazers, women in brocade saris, gold and diamond sparkling at high tea. In the mothers, as they greeted mine, I saw, year after year, the same false sympathies; in each of the smiling fathers, I saw a murderer.

As soon as I could leave, I decided, I would leave. I'd go away as far as I could. Distance would be my antidote.

But what was I doing here, pulled over? Wasn't there more to it than the vaulting salaries, the bonuses, than my success? Was I a well-intentioned, self-appointed sleuth or a seeker, the fatherless son, the offspring Bernstein never had? Except for that one evening at Benford's?

Except, in a manner, each day, in the office opposite his?

Bernstein, as it turned out, was well. "But he's done," said Panorama's general counsel on the phone. The company board had known since the weekend.

Now was my turn to be told. Would I stay on to help close the fund? Would I, at Bernstein's personal request, help oversee his apartment's sale?

Where was he?

I thought of Bernstein on a yacht, strange as it appeared, off the Caymans or the Canaries. Like an act in a play, it had been all planned out. He'd told no one, but the moment, he'd known, would come. He knew I would be there to help. He'd decide early morning, midday, late in the night, just like that: I'm done.

And why not? The investors had much to be thankful for.

Their money had multiplied, the longest ones' many times over.

A windfall, once again, awaited me.

Maybe it was luck, maybe it was not.

I was still in the car. "Stop by my office in an hour," the counsel said.

*

Late Sunday morning, the air brisk, the streets already abuzz.

Upstairs, the wallpapered foyer, a pattern of striped gilt and teal; a bureau; the intercom. To the right, Bernstein's study.

A large, maple desk near the center of the room faced the door, behind it a window opened west. A notebook, leather frayed and wrinkled, was propped against the lamp. I thumbed it. The last page had a quote: *But as for me, I will walk in mine integrity: redeem me, and be merciful unto me.*

On the hutch was a large diary. I flipped through it. I found the entry with my name, my number, those of my colleagues, of others I recognized, associates, clients. I stopped at a familiar name. I called the number.

The voice was brusque: Hi, this is Betty.

"I haven't seen him in years," she said, "or heard from him."

She had known him for two years. They had met early in the summer, gone to shows, private book launches and art openings, dined at Benford's. It was promising, until, until… She paused. She wasn't quite clear what had happened. She had found him becoming increasingly self-absorbed, felt him distant. He wanted more and more to be left alone.

She liked to talk. I didn't interrupt. She was materializing in my mind. White hair, wavy, neat with a touch of unruliness. Urbanely gritty, but sensitive, probably a single mother, a widow or a divorcee for longer than she'd care to bring up, ten years, fifteen. She volunteered at a nonprofit, or, as a docent, at a museum. I imagined her barefoot in the kitchen, brunch in oven, aperitif in one hand, phone in the other, the Sunday *New York Times* spread on the counter. Once, she said, they went to the cemetery where his wife is buried, a few miles from where he spent his weekends upstate. Then, at her insistence, he took her to meet his daughter, Sara.

Afternoon light came in through the window. Outside it flooded the rooftop of the Metropolitan Museum, fell slantwise on the walls of surrounding buildings.

"I hope he's alright," she said.

3

My father's life's a lacuna despite the frequent dreams. He mostly appears blurred, as in the black-and-white, matte photo I carry in my wallet of a man younger than I am now, lean, shirtless in swimming trunks and thick glasses, hair short and wavy, reclined on a beach chair, legs crossed. The image is dark, almost a silhouette against the silvery sea. I have to look closely to make out features. The dreams extrapolate from that snapshot, the years before, the handful of years after: the dreams in which he appears younger than in the photo lead to the man in the photo; the dreams in which he appears older, evolve from the photo. When I wake up in the middle of the night, I write down what I recall of the dream. I should by now, after all these years, have conjured a life that's fully outlined, even if it's fiction.

But the man who emerges from my notes is contradictory; his story unravels, he becomes conundrum, the son, shy and modest, of an honest, underpaid government employee, but also a competitive, trailblazing company man with a corner office. A devoted and responsible husband and father, but also reckless, as one might judge from the photo, cigarette in a hand that dangles lazily down, almost touching the sand, as if, handsome, with dark eyes, and carefree, he were a lothario. Again and again I disassemble and reassemble him, seeking a clean story. Again and again I dream and write him down, a life, pivoted in the photo, in his mid-twenties, that's larger than a whole life, even as, like a log of spruce, he burned fast.

Some, like hawthorn, burn slowly, the flame working its way unnoticed until all that's left is mostly ash. Bernstein, to those who knew him professionally, wasn't much more than a persona. The occasions to notice were few, and no one saw the mask recede into the self any more than anyone noticed him lean back in a chair. I thought I saw once, for a moment, at Benford's. But he was too good an actor, didn't betray his role.

It was the weather, I said to myself, the want for a drive out of the city, for quiet, that impelled me to be at the cemetery. I parked outside the undertaker's office, and walked past the synagogue, across the manicured lawns with elms and willows and a gazebo, to the grave. It was not, I said to myself, the hope of meeting Bernstein. He was already becoming ghost: no sign of a person, though he had been there. A fresh bouquet lay by his wife's headstone, crocuses and anemones around asters, heleniums, and sunflowers.

I drove the few miles to the New York Institute of Neurological Disorders, to which I was to ensure the transfer of proceeds from the sale of Bernstein's penthouse. I pulled up on the curb outside the park adjacent to the campus. A metal fence separated the public and private properties. I walked along it down toward the Hudson riverfront, piers north and south in the distance, past a stone building mid-slope some yards behind the fence.

I heard clamor.

A group of women in single file, escorted by attendants in uniform, were leaving the building. Some in wheelchairs, some of them pushed, they settled halfway down the slope. Another group followed them, then another, another. Once together, they mingled on the lawn. The youngest was adolescent, the eldest middle-aged. Sheets were laid out on the grass, a lemonade stand set up. The wards who could, sat on the lawn. Some jumped, some clapped. The movements of some were constrained and exaggerated, arms turning in twisted arcs through the air. One started to sway back and forth on the ground. One wept. One struck her face.

One of them was Sara Bernstein.

*

Bernstein's last gift to me, his last day at the office, was tickets for a play. *American Buffalo*. David Mamet. I watched it over the weekend. Afterward, I sat at the bar at Pablo's on Ninth Avenue and drank a beer.

I'd never regretted the move to Panorama. I'd liked Bernstein immediately, even during the interview. He'd never made me feel I needed to be someone else, something else, to be better; I was fine as I was. He'd kept his word, let me define my role at the firm over the years.

When Angus's position had again opened up for me, I'd

turned it down. But not only because I'd just been hired by Bernstein.

"We've known each other for a couple of years now," the recruiter had said, "so I can be candid with you. I think you're making a big, big mistake leaving Delta. Reconsider."

Angus, everyone had started to note, would shut the door to his office minutes after the last partner had left for the day. Soon, music would blare from the boombox inside. Then he'd open the door, step out, and dance down the hall, then up, and back and forth, humming and singing. But not until a high-profile client, after losing a small fortune at Delta, insisted on an urgent meeting with the partners—with everyone's counsels present—did anyone talk about Angus's having had to be escorted out of the Oak Lounge during a business meeting earlier that month.

"Did you know about it?" one of the partners asked. "About the cocaine?" We were in the conference room with the board, the lawyers.

"No," I said.

I'd watched them from the time they'd lured me to the firm after giving my job to Angus. I'd detested more and more each day their easy manner, their shiny wingtips, their dyed hair, their lies.

I will walk, he'd written, *in mine integrity*. Bernstein's masterwork, I thought, was his life, calibrated so perfectly in public, it seemed flawless, that he seemed flawless, with his subtle charm on TV, at Benford's, in meetings with clients.

I'd be at the office early on Monday and start steadily unwinding the trades. The day, I thought, would be shorter than it was two weeks ago; soon, it would be winter.

I thought of what I'd do next, after Panorama was

shuttered. I'd maybe start my own firm, ask Oscar to work for me. He'd agree.

I'd have to be careful, I thought. The trade that had not gone through would have wiped out Panorama. Bernstein would never have approved it, would have seen right through it. It was too complicated.

MEIN BRUDER

1

"I met our father here for the first time," said Gabriele out-side the Siegessäule. "I was twenty-six."

It was August, hot and cloudless. The city stood recessed beyond the avenues that converged to the road circling the tower. The column and, atop it, the statue of Victoria were foreshortened in an angled shadow behind us that swept the cars that arced and sped by.

"'Time heals all,'" I said, "'but what if time itself is the disease?'"

"*Der Himmel über Berlin*," she said, recalling the Wim Wenders film. *Wings of Desire*. I had watched it, subtitled in English, earlier that summer on her recommendation.

She took out a photo from her handbag. "See," she said, turning her head to the side and holding out from the back a cluster of wavy hair, "there was no gray then." It showed her father and she, twenty-five years ago to the date, to the hour, sitting on the stairs where we were sitting, on a day not dissimilar to this one, both in sunglasses, papa's white linen blazer draped over his knee, she in a long, pink dress.

"The same dress?"

"Yes." She stretched her legs, raised them, swept a hand over the creases between the pleats, straightened them. She flapped the skirt, the hem fell again over her calves.

She had shown her father—our father—her family

photos, the early ones in black-and-white, of herself as a girl, of her mother, of her sisters, of her son Anton, whose father, a painter of abstract canvases in acrylics and oils, had left her when she was pregnant. First it was my father, she said; then it was my boyfriend. She sat quietly for a while and looked ahead. "Unlike my mother," she said, "I did not hold a grudge against my father: he, after all, gave me life. I would have liked to be by his side when he passed, but I understood the complications, the… decorum?… the decorum one must maintain in society, especially when one has an important career, when one has worked so hard to, to…"

Every so often she groped for the correct words: when one has worked so hard, she meant to say, to burnish an unblemished image. "But toward Anton's father," she said, "I am angry, even after thirty years, because of what he did to me and especially to Anton."

She and I were for the first time together both away from our homes, both travelers in a city, a cosmopolitan place and not, as it were, some cloistered or provincial one. The surroundings had unfettered her, I thought, and she, never loquacious, now felt unreserved. The occasion, too, with its flood of memory, perhaps inspired her to express herself, to share uninhibitedly her thoughts with the one person, now beside her, to whom it mattered.

An aura of stillness, even with the tourists and the traffic, surrounded the concourse. Parks flanked the roads, spectrums of green dense with trees and foliage.

"After I found our father," she said, "I was excited to learn about you. I hoped one day to find you, but then, shortly thereafter, your letter arrived. Anton, he, you, and me never dined together as I dreamed we would, at a handsome restaurant in Munich or New York or in a canteen off the sidewalk in Istanbul or Lisbon, but I am thankful for sharing a meal with our father here, at this very spot. He had brought two döners and two bottles of Coca-Cola. After we ate, he took a book out from his satchel and opened it. 'This statuette,' he said, pointing to a picture, 'is here, in the Pergamonmuseum. Let's go there.'

"It was a weekday: the Underground was crowded, the galleries were not. We found the piece—a Mesopotamian relic—then walked down the Processional Way to the Ishtar Gate in the south wing. We stood before it. I could not understand..." She shook her head so her hair fell over her face, and held out some strands and looked at them. "I could not understand how anyone could have stood attentive for as long as he did, even before such a beautiful creation. I felt troubled that I, with whom he had engaged so meaningfully until then, was no longer the center of his attention. I had ceased to exist, and the museum, too, had ceased to exist for him, and he stared as if, I thought, he was an ancient traveler in Babylon in the sixth century BC. A part of me understood: Anton's father used to become like that in front of the Rembrandts in the Rijksmuseum, the Rothkos and the Turners in the Tate Gallery. But a part of me did not understand: this was a special occasion.

"Our father was gazing at a bas relief of an auroch when, finally, I asked him, shall I meet you somewhere later? He did not answer, and I asked him again, louder, 'Shall we meet later?' He turned, surprised, as if he had been woken from a slumber, or had been unexpectedly accosted by a stranger, and said, 'Yes,' but not unkindly, in fact with a gentleness I had not sensed before, 'that's a terrific idea.'

"'Where?'

"'Oh, anywhere.'

"'At the museum café?'

"'Yes.' He looked at his watch. 'Let's meet half an hour before they close so we can eat something.' He must have sensed my disappointment. 'Wait,' he said, 'take this before I forget.' He opened the book in his hand and inscribed it. On the cover was a reproduction of a William Blake etching of Nebuchadnezzer, below it the title, *Between Mythology and Art*. Below that was his name. Thank you, I said, looking up—I was beaming—I feel honored, but he had already turned around and was walking away. He waved to me without turning, and whether it meant, see you soon, or whether it was a gesture to dismiss me I could not tell. He was suddenly no longer the person I had sat with here, at the Siegessäule, an hour earlier. His hair was muffled, he had lost the care and attention of the well-groomed man in the photo in your hand. His shirt was untucked in the back, his jacket, wrapped over his arm, was scraping the floor. I started to walk back down the Way. I turned once to look at him. He stood as before, farther down the hall, staring at the ancient blue enamel.

"Before five, I bought from the museum shop for him a postcard with an image of a detail from the Way, of a lion. Then I sat in the café until it closed, then waited outside for an hour. I wanted to fill out the postcard and mail it to him, but I could not write, my hand was shaking. The buildings on Museuminsel had emptied, their shadows, dribbling down the stairs, had started to fade. The last of the visitors had dispersed across the Spree. At night I called his hotel from my dear friend Agnes's apartment. I was told there was no guest by his name. Over the months, I wrote him letter after letter from wherever I was. I was restless, traveled a lot. I must have written one hundred letters. When I opened the book a few days later on the train home, I knew from the references and illustrations that he was familiar not just with the statuette, but also with the Gate, and in fact with a large part of the museum's collection, if not all of it. That he remained so oblivious to my—his daughter's—presence in the museum despite there being on display nothing novel, so to speak, disillusioned me more, considering especially that I had emerged alive in his life while the museum was artefacts, inanimate, dead."

Gabriele and I had started to walk. She was silent as we left the traffic behind us. In the park, on Kastanienallee, among the horse chestnuts, a mosaic of light and shadow around us, she looked down as if measuring her steps. When she spoke again, she gazed ahead. "You probably do not know these things," she said. "Until now, the only other person who knew was Agnes. I have always felt close to her since we met in the gymnasium. She even looks now how my mother used to look, and the closeness I feel to her I feel to no one else. When we separated to go to different universities, I was lonely. Nothing I read at that time made less deep the abyss before me, made less dark the darkness. I could forget the meaninglessness of life only with Anton's father, untouched as he is by the mysteries that have obsessed philosophers and poets."

I, too, remembered that summer, unextraordinary but for its milestone to the winter that followed, making it a year of record snowfall in the northeast, when I drove to my parents' from Massachusetts to Rhode Island for the holidays barely exceeding twenty miles per hour on Interstate 495, gusts rattling the car. The house was desolate, more so at dusk, and more so beside the lit-up porches of the neighbors. Unlike in past years, there were no decorations in the front yard, none on the trees, none on the door. Papa had no colleagues over, and when my mother's friends came, he stayed in the attic, which had become an annex to his study. He had had a large mahogany desk placed there in the fall and was spending most of his days hunched over it in a thick overcoat, and sometimes a hat, and sleeping in the dankness on a sofa whose springs were long kaput.

He was working on something—I couldn't tell what—annotating critical editions of Herodotus and Xenophon, a new translation of Gilgamesh, the poems of Gerard Manley Hopkins. He had gained weight, grown a beard, not had a haircut in three months.

I stayed until midweek before I returned to Boston to conduct a winter session seminar at Emerson College. As I was leaving, he waddled, slouched like a thief, to the driveway and handed me a badly gift-wrapped shoebox from under his unbuttoned coat. It contained her letters, envelopes—cheap hotel stationery—with stamps from Europe, from Germany, Poland, Italy, France, the addresses handwritten. Those that arrived later, he forwarded to me unopened.

*

"When is Anton back?" I asked on the Metro to Charlottenburg. We were staying at Agnes's, where we had arrived that morning, Gabriele from Bonn, I from Boston. The building on one side rose above a courtyard shared by an elementary school and a church. A stone clock tower loomed, dial white, hands and Roman digits gilt.

"I don't know. He's still in Asia. He loves photography, you know? He said he needs to see new things, to feel… to be…"

"Astonished?"

"Astonished?"

"Surprised. Shocked, in a good way, out of the status

quo. Where in Asia?" We were on an elevated stretch of the U-Bahn, standing and holding the overhead handrail. It was rush hour, the train crowded. Her brow was beaded with sweat. The sun sloughed off the commuters as we approached a station.

She removed a cellphone from her bag and scrolled though the messages. "Yesterday," she said, "he was in Vientiane, two days before that in Mandalay, two days before that in Colombo. Tomorrow, who knows?" He had left in July when his father was to be in Bonn for a month-long residency and an exhibition of his drawings at the famous Durchdenwald Kunstgalerie.

"He hates his father," she said. "He hates him more than anything."

Shafts of light flashed inside as the train pulled out of the station.

2

"Do you know any German?" asked Agnes.

We were at a table on the sidewalk on Kantstrasse outside Neue Phuket, under a large umbrella advertising Gerolsteiner. She refilled our glasses, placed the wine bottle in the ice bucket. On her arm, as it bent, six inches of amethysts, carnelians, and bloodstones slid to her elbow.

The crest of summer. A foreign city. A neighborhood serene and grand. Before me, the sun hovered above the crenellated roof across the street. I savored the light, an emollient on my face, and felt an ease one can know only when it has long been elusive. Just days ago, I had started to see how my essays would organize themselves in the book that—with the research, the travel, the interviews, the stretches of days in libraries, nights in the office—had now

75

wrangled me for two years, how the chapters, the photographs, the oral histories had aligned as if to a natural sequence, a preordained pattern of a critical account of the 1947 Partition of India, one of the greatest atrocities of the previous century, the barbaric end of a barbaric occupation that left a nation fractured, two million dead, and twenty million displaced.

"*Danke schoen*," I said, "*guten Appetit, gute Nacht, mein Bruder*." The waiter was negotiating his way, laying out the dishes. "*Sehnsucht*." Before us lay rolls, rice, steamed vegetables, seafood.

"Anton must be eating a lot of this nowadays," said Gabriele.

"What does it mean, *sehnsucht*?"

"Desire."

"It has no equivalent in English."

"Longing."

"No." Her eyes were round, her face freckled, lips ruddy. Brunette, her hair not short, not long, was wavy. It curled unevenly over her forehead. Professional by necessity, she was otherwise careless, her fridge empty, her coffee instant. She drank it black.

"I'm sorry my flat is such a mess," she said as we walked after dinner past the majestic houses on Witzlebenplatz, into the park along the promenade along the Lietzensee. At some point between when we were introduced and that moment, I had started to matter enough for her to care about the appearance of her apartment. At the waterfront, off the Beer Garden, was the large stump of a Mammut tree burnt by lightning. "Before, I used to sit beneath it and read," a practice, I would learn later that evening, that underscored her disappointment with men. They, in her experience, were either too cerebral—and appreciated such solitary escapades, but were themselves, too, withdrawn—or not at all. Either way, they were hopeless.

Buildings rose from beyond the lindens and the planes along the lake and surrounding streets; statues emerged along the path from beyond the branches. "Wistfulness," I proposed, as we drew out a thread earlier cut short in a three-way conversation. Gabriele had gone back to the apartment to speak with Anton and Bernhard and turn in. The following day, starting early, she would be visiting friends settled in various boroughs.

No, it had no English equivalent, Agnes again insisted. She had a glint in her eyes, relished the upper hand, and, after years abroad completing a PhD in renewable energy at Berkeley, still had the zeal of a proud native. She led me down Friedbergstrasse with its striking yet understated architectural motifs: the ornate moldings around the doors and windows, the triangular roofs, the projections of balconies, the juxtapositions, arresting even at dusk as the streetlamps turned on, of muted colors. "It's Belle Époque," she said, "1890s to 1920s. Berlin was built in those three or four decades."

In the dark, an otherworldly fluorescence from the res-taurants at the intersection across Stuttgarter Platz reflected from the sidewalk, from the women and men in dresses and blazers dining outside. She'd join me, she said, but first she'd go home and change.

When we left, it was close to midnight. Gabriele was asleep on the sofa. From my room—an alcove, Agnes's study—a small balcony overlooked the courtyard, the clock tower blanched in moonlight. Beige chiffon curtains rustled in the breeze, skimming the desk. I lay down on the futon. The evening, unraveling, spooled before me: the avenues, the houses; Billie Holiday, sad and mellifluous, husky

through Gasthaus Mendelssohn; the cognac, warm, trans-
lucent, and gold, its bouquet still on my nose; the varnished
walnut table, the candle between us—Agnes, in a sleeve-
less, lapis blue dress, and me—the rims of our snifters
flickering rings in its glow.

*

Sheets of amber sifted through scattered clouds, white and
luminous, ablaze at the edges. The streets, early Saturday,
were empty, cool. We walked to the Charlottenburg Palace
and, the museums yet to open, to the park behind it, up the
tree-lined promenade and back along the Spree, aqua-
marine, rippling, stray leaves adrift on the surface.

The night had brought about an unspoken familiarity, as
if this were a reunion. "And what do you see in this?" she
asked, pointing down from the winding stairs as we
descended from the Picasso galleries. A Giacometti sculp-
ture stood under the skylight in the center of the foyer.

"A tragic century."

"All centuries are tragic."

The sun had chiseled its way through the streets when we
left the Berggruen Museum. The light was unfiltered, the
temperature in the nineties. I carried both our sweaters. She
closed her eyes, turned her head to the glare. Stones rattled,
slid down her arm as she opened her eyes and shielded them
with her hand; they slid again when she looped her arm
around mine.

"Tomorrow," she said, "back to work." She was present-
ing a paper at a conference the following week.

"Why work Sundays to save a planet that's fucked?"

"Let's go home for lunch."

What about the Ethiopian place she'd pointed out earlier?

"No, I want to cook."

"You don't cook."

"Wait and see."

Along the way, she had a change of heart and we stopped for takeout at a Lebanese imbiss. "It'll taste home-cooked," she said, "in my grandmother's porcelain."

*

The beam of light from the window splashed over Agnes. It cast her profile on the carpet, where I lay in shadow, half asleep. The ceiling was decorated here and there with elaborately embossed and engraved period tiles. "Your apartment looks both old and new."

"Is that good or bad?"

"Both baroque and spartan."

"Is that good or bad?"

"Catholic and Protestant…"

"Both, yes, I get your point."

"It's good. *Sehr gut*."

She was sitting up, perusing the museum catalogue she'd bought. "What do you think of this one?"

I turned and propped my head. "It's very playful." Her toenails, painted turquoise, matched her top.

"Like a child's drawing, no?" She contemplated it attentively, then flipped through the pages. "I should learn to make art."

"What would you paint?"

"I don't know. Maybe fruits," she said, "in a bowl. But first I would have to buy some fruits." She laughed. "What are you looking at?"

"Your crow's feet."

There was a silence. It stunned. The music, the hum of

the air-conditioner, faded. Our breaths wafted above it. She was shaking. Her hair was warm.

I had shut my eyes. Outside, the avenues smoldered, the awnings of storefronts melted. The cars, the pedestrians, receded. The church bell, at the hour, didn't ring.

We were awoken by shouts of children in the courtyard.

Later, her fingers curled around mine, we walked to Karl-August-Platz, where Gabriele would be meeting us for dinner.

I heard them whispering in German that night till I fell asleep.

3

Four hundred years after the beginning of the Thirty Years' War, two hundred after Napoleon's march through the Brandenburg Gate, a century after the Great War, the city, its sapphire halo the color of bruise, slept.

It had rained at night. On a tree, a kestrel sang. In sandals, I felt the chill on my feet, the pavement's dewy vapor. History had distilled to that unadulterated moment, peaceful and immaculate; it showed no imprint of troubled epochs, of the blood of Europe.

Agnes had left already. Soon she would be at a desk in a modern office with glass walls, hazy behind a film of condensation, face aglow behind a lamp.

The whirr of a derailleur sharpened as a cyclist rode past me, silence in his wake.

Café Kloster, its exterior of stone, hadn't quite opened, but the wrought-iron gate and heavy wooden door were ajar. Face to the entrance, the waitress had her head on an arm stretched across the back corner table. She yawned. I sat by a window, its louvered shutters open. I thumbed my travel guide. She grudgingly moved, turned on the coffee machine, the lights above the empty cake displays at the bar.

Gabriele would join me presently. At dinner she had insisted I repeat the day's tour—the schloss, the museum—this time with her. I had agreed. After that, we would go to the Pergamonmuseum.

She's very possessive of you, Agnes had said, she talks about you every time we talk. No, I had said, she's very possessive of you.

Below the ceilings along the wall was a medieval frieze replica. I made out, to my left in the corner, the Annunciation, to the right, the Magi. The narrative uncoiled around me.

Suddenly I felt repulsed by the kitsch interior, by the plaster Ionic pillar behind the bar, its surface artificially marbleized, its fake capital with a volute.

Outside, the buildings were surrendering their secrets, sunlight defining their edges, their dimensions, carving out their facades. I downed an espresso, ordered another. When she arrived, the breads, the Berliners, the eggs, the cheeses were at the table. She sat down without a word.

The indictment was quick, the verdict irrevocable: I would leave immediately. She moved the spoon around the rim of her cup slowly, collecting the froth at the edge, and put it in her mouth without looking up. "You're just like your father," she said.

*

I knew what would ensue: years of silence, the chasm between us too wide for a lifetime to bridge. Maybe there would be reconciliation when we were old, by which time remorse, yet to incubate, would have ripened and clutched us, unshakable.

I was nursing a nightcap at a bar in Marzahn. It had multicolored track lighting and loud pop music. It was empty except for the bartender and me.

I looked up across the street toward my room in the pension where I had checked in that morning. Nondescript, concrete, gray, it was a relic of the East from the days of the Wall.

I thought of Gabriele at the other end of the city, on the sofa in the living room; Agnes, in a white chemise, sat beside her. The French doors of the study and of its balcony were open, my sheets rumpled and streaked by shadows, moonlight spilling on the futon.

I thought of my forthcoming meeting with my publisher, Felix Biesinger, the following week in Frankfurt, of the informal celebration of my book's completion he was hosting in his house. I had called him that afternoon to let him know I was in Germany. He had just returned from a long vacation in Ireland, but was miffed. "The distributor," he said, "is refusing to accept *The British Holocaust* as the English edition's title."

"Why?"

"One of the board member's a Brit."

I thought of Aantya Huq, the reclusive avant-garde film-maker in Calcutta, now ninety, with whom Felix had arranged an interview, and whom I had met two months ago. Before other scholars had rushed, decades later, to compile oral histories of the Partition, she had captured firsthand accounts from survivors on film and edited short documentaries, some of which had been broadcast on national television.

Her house was a vestige of grandeur. The outside walls were patinized by wear, splotched black behind the tall, dusty palms that extended above the three-story structure. She occupied the entire first floor, a few steps above the compound, the interior resplendent in light and space, vigorous in color and contrast, walls a mellow, matted mustard, large exposures, sills and doorframes glossed burgundy. The floors were black-and-white checkered tiles, visibly chipped, the furniture colonial, teak and wicker.

In 1946, she said, when she was sixteen, her father, a doctor of some reputation, had anticipated the intensification of sectarian violence—in hindsight there were signs of its upsurge everywhere in the north—and had managed, with the help of one of his patients, to secure accommodation for his family on a Royal Navy ship to Bombay by bribing a British officer. Soon, she said, my father's mother, already fragile, got seasick, and a day into the journey, she died. The sea was tranquil the morning after, light-specked ripples all around in consistent, perpetual motion so as to seem motionless, the sky clear, the sun blazing across the water all the way to the horizon. I remember my grandmother's body laid out on the deck's stern swathed in white, of my father on his knees, hands clasped, pleading with the captain not to toss the corpse overboard, to preserve it on board until we docked, for the last rites. But the captain just nodded, stiff, unfazed. It's because of you, I screamed, butcher, we have to make this journey, but he would have none of it and asked for my mother to take me away. But she didn't move. She stared at him defiantly, indignant, standing beside my father. I stepped back and grabbed the taffrail in case he instructed one of his crew to take me away, and glared at him, in utmost hatred, which I could not conceal. I remember his red-splotched, mustached face, his near-bald head, a limey, not quite my father's age, in uniform. Finally, he asked my father to his cabin. The corpse was placed in the onboard morgue, for, I learned later, an exorbitant bribe.

Each day we met, Huq, her eyes flared, repeated the story, both at the beginning and at the end of our conversations. I had not approached her for an oral history, but I realized, as we spoke, hers would be incorporated, and complement others in the book. But what about her art?

Shortly after we arrived, she said, my father set up a medical practice in the south of the city, an area known as Fort, not far from where we rented a furnished flat. I still remember the sweet and putrid odor of the clinic. I still remember the location, close to the Bombay Stock Exchange, a street off Horniman Circle with its spectacular colonial buildings, the main road straight ahead with horse carriages back and forth past the gorgeous High Victorian Gothic building of Saint Sebastian College, ethereal with the gaslights lit at night. One afternoon soon thereafter, my life changed when an American woman about the age of my mother walked into the clinic to have treated a bruise on her hand, her palm bleeding as a result of a fall. She was carrying cameras and bags, straps slung over her shoulders. She seemed fearless, and smiled and winked at me as my father cleaned and dressed the wound. Why aren't you in school? she asked. How old are you? I was sixteen, waiting for the new term to begin before I could resume my studies. She let me play with her cameras and showed me photographs. I'll be traveling all over the country, she said. Would you like to join me?

I begged my parents to let me go. The photographer, whom they invited home for dinner, reassured them. It would be the experience of a lifetime for a young woman, she said. Eventually, they acceded, but mostly on account of my mother. She herself had been a trailblazer as the first girl accepted to her secondary school when it had become coeducational, and, even after I was born, had wished for herself a bohemian life. Also, unlike my father, she had heard of the photographer, Margaret Bourke-White.

I accompanied her to many of the locations of her photographs. With her I witnessed the horrors of slaughters, hangings, molestations, and rapes, right here, in and around Calcutta, where I've been, more or less, ever since. Margaret had been everywhere, she had been to Nazi Germany, and she called the Partition a Buchenwald. You, said Huq, reaching for the glass of lemonade on the coffee table and taking a sip, should call your book *The British Buchenwald*. Her brow furrowed. She took another sip, set down the glass.

I postponed school for a year, she continued, but I never went back. What good is education, anyway? It's true test is in its efficacy and fortitude in the face of reality at its far fringes, and beyond them, where reality becomes more unreal than anything anyone imagines. There, education has shown itself to be speechless and impotent. My one short film reveals more about human depravity than all textbooks consumed for three or four or five years at any university. I once said that to your father, like you, a professor. He understood. He was dedicated to scholarship, but was open-minded, always evolving. It's a miracle you exist, I never imagined him marrying. I was influenced and inspired by his work. I was older when I met him, and already making films, whose possibilities I started to explore after Margaret left. I taught myself the craft, and for much of my practice, my subject has been only the Partition and its roots in the occupation. Of my family, including my late husband, I have no footage.

At the end of the week, when we concluded the interview, once more she repeated the account of her family's migration. "I'll never forget the captain," she said as I turned off the recorder and put away the stationery, "I'll never forget his filthy face." She walked me down the hall and affectionately clasped my outstretched hand with both of hers. "He was just another…," she said, waving as she shut the door, "another worthless, toothless limey, like the rest."

Outside, cars dashed across the former Eastern Bloc roads. The bowl of the glass of brandy, its stem between my fingers, was warm. The bar was bustling. Drafts of heat blasted in as people entered and left. The air conditioner rattled ineffectively. I thought, in the balminess, of anger—not only Gabriele's, not only Huq's—but anger—rage, undying, elemental rage—bred everywhere of human folly, amplified to collective folly, to the follies of societies, of nations, of the world, follies that, in their wake, destroyed and bred more anger. I felt resigned to our condition, in all its grotesque permutations, and in that resignation perceived an assuring, comforting clarity of our futility, of the asinine simplicity of our lives, doomed, inevitably, as we were, unable to confront folly—folly encountered from without, folly engendered from within. A startingly modest conclusion, I thought: our unalterable fate was chaos. I fathomed this epiphany under the gaudy lights, the awful music blaring around me, not as an ecstatic religious vision, but, as an academic might in a lucid moment, as a logical, universal theory: everything folly, unopposable. Perhaps, I thought, my father understood this, and turned his attention to art for its dignity, for enterprise that stood against unrest and vanity, and endured through disappointments, through hatreds, through disasters, through pogroms, wars, civilizations.

I thought, too, of Anton, in Hanoi or in Okinawa, his own

rage in remission. The world was opening its secrets to him as he treaded old pavements in Birkenstocks. He took his backpack off every now and then to sit for a cup of tea or a bowl of noodles. Here it was night, but there it was dawn, cool in the drizzle. Camera in hand, he was walking in the mist past the statue of a man on horseback, across a quiet, empty cobblestone square once wracked by shelling or an earthquake, toward an odd building on the periphery that, while everything around it crumbled, had somehow escaped ruin.

ACKNOWLEDGMENTS

I thank the following friends, exacting critics: Stefania Amfitheatrof, Nicholas Birns, Adil Jussawalla, Graziano Krätli, Richard Manley, and Tayve Neese. The stories in this collection are aged with their insights.

Good fortune led me, an undergraduate at Cornell University, to Robert Morgan and Michael Koch, who early on cultivated my interest in fiction, especially in the short story; Keith Hjortshoj primed the underclassman for their workshops. I thank them all.

I am grateful to my publisher Hal Hartley for making this book and for his dedication to Elboro Press.

Words fail my immense gratitude to my family, from whom my journey—at home, in exile; in attendance, in absentia; in verse, in prose—began.

BB